THE BOY RANCHERS ON THE TRAIL

OR

The Diamond X After Cattle Rustlers

WILLARD F. BAKER

1st WORLD LIBRARY
Literary Society

The Boy Ranchers on the Trail

Willard F. Baker

© 1st World Library – Literary Society, 2004
PO Box 2211
Fairfield, IA 52556
www.1stworldlibrary.org
First Edition

LCCN: 2004195369

Softcover ISBN: 1-59540-808-8
Hardcover ISBN: 1-59540-803-7
eBook ISBN: 1-59540-813-4

Purchase *"The Boy Ranchers on the Trail"*
as a traditional bound book at:
www.1stWorldLibrary.org/purchase.asp?ISBN=1-59540-808-8

1st World Library Literary Society is a nonprofit
organization dedicated to promoting literacy by:

- Creating a free internet library accessible from any
  computer worldwide.
- Hosting writing competitions and offering book
  publishing scholarships.

Readers interested in supporting literacy
through sponsorship, donations or
membership please contact:
literacy@1stworldlibrary.org
Check us out at: www.1stworldlibrary.ORG
and start downloading free ebooks today.

The Boy Ranchers on the Trail
contributed by Tim, Ed & Rodney
in support of
1st World Library Literary Society

CONTENTS

CHAPTER I

THE ROUND-UP

"Come on, Nort! It's your turn to cut out the next one!"

"S'pose I make a mux of it, Bud!"

"Shucks! You won't do that! You've roped a calf before!"

"Yes, but not at a big round-up like this. If I make a fizzle the fellows will give me the laugh!"

"What if they do? Everybody knows you haven't been at it long, and you've got to make a start. Besides, anybody's likely to make a mistake. That's why they put rubbers on the ends of pencils. Ride in now and snake out the next one, Nort!"

"All right, Bud! Here goes!"

Blaze, the pony Nort Shannon was riding toward the bunch of cattle gathered at Diamond X ranch for the big, spring round-up, leaped forward at the sound of his master's voice, and in response to the little jerk of the reins and the clap of heels against his sides. Into the herd of milling, turning and twisting cattle the intelligent animal made his way, needing hardly any guidance from Nort. The lad, by a mere touch, corrected the course of Blaze slightly, and in a moment he was heading for a calf which bawled loudly.

"Get him, Nort!" cried a voice from among the cowboys looking on.

"Don't get me fussed, Dick!" Nort shouted back to his brother, who sat astride his pony near Bud Merkle. "It'll be your turn next!"

Into the herd he wormed his way on Blaze, dodging here and there, but with his eyes ever on the calf he hoped to cut out so it could be branded. Nort leaned forward in his saddle, and then his cousin and brother, eagerly watching from outside the herd, saw the boy rancher's hand shoot up.

Through the air the rope went, turning, twisting, writhing and uncoiling like a snake. In an instant it had flipped around the hind legs of a calf.

"Good!" yelled Dick.

"Even Babe couldn't 'a' done better!" complimented Bud, enthusiastically.

"'Tisn't over yet!" gasped Nort, for he had hard work ahead of him, and the dust raised by thousands of hoofs was choking. "Wait 'till I get it to the branding corral!"

He leaned over in his other stirrup, causing the lariat to pull taut and, the next instant the calf flopped on its side.

"Snake him out, Blaze!" cried Nort to his pony, and the animal turned and dragged the prostrate calf along over the ground, an operation not as cruel as it sounds as the surface was inches thick in soft dust, like flour.

"That's the boy, Nort!" called his cousin Bud. "I knew you could do it! Now then, Dick! Let's see how you'll make out!"

"I can't throw a rope as good as Nort," answered the stouter lad, as he urged his pony, Blackie, into the herd. "But here goes!"

Meanwhile Nort had dragged the calf he had cut out to the corral where the branding was going on. Two cowboys, stationed there for the purpose, leaped forward and threw the calf over on its side, for it had managed to struggle to its feet when Nort ceased dragging it. One man twisted a front leg of the struggling creature back in a hammerlock and knelt on its neck. The other took hold of the upper hind leg, and with this hold prevented the calf from sprawling along on the ground.

"Sit on him!" called Mr. Merkel, owner of Diamond X and other ranches. He was superintending the round-up of his herds and those entrusted to Bud, Nort and Dick in the first business venture of the boy ranchers. "Sit on him!" yelled Bud's father.

Accordingly the men sat on the calf, thus, with the holds they had secured, keeping it under restraint with the least possible pain to the small creature.

"Branding iron!" sang out Slim Degnan, foreman of the ranch.

A little blaze was flickering on the ground, not far from where the calf Nort had cut out was thrown and held. In a moment the fire-tender had seized the branding iron, and, a second or two later, it was being pressed on the calf's flank.

The creature bawled loudly, and kicked out, thereby nearly throwing off the men who were sitting on it. But the branding was all over in a moment, and the men leaped up, releasing the animal.

The calf stood, dazed for the time being, after it had scrambled to its feet, and then trotted out of the corral, lashing its side with its little tail. Plainly branded on it now, never to be completely effaced, was the mark of the ownership of Mr. Merkel - an X inside a diamond.

"Next!" called the branders:

"Here comes Dick!" shouted Bud, as Nort rode up beside him. "And he got his calf!" "Good!" exclaimed the brother. "I guess we're learning the business!"

"Surest thing you know!" asserted the son of the owner of Diamond X. "I told you it wasn't so hard, and you've done the same thing before."

"But not at such a big round-up," remarked Nort, as he prepared to ride in again and cut out another calf.

"Yes, it is big," admitted Bud, as he made ready for his share in the affair - his task being the same as that of his cousins - to cut out the calves for branding purposes. "It sure is a big round-up."

It had been in progress for days. Twice a year on the

big, western ranches, the cattle are driven in from the outlying ranges, to be tallied, inspected, marked and shipped away. The spring and fall round-ups are always busy seasons at any ranch.

During the times between round-ups the new calves attained their growth, but they needed to have branded into their hides the marks of their owners. Then, too, some yearlings escaped branding at times, either by remaining out of sight at the round-up, or in the attending confusion.

Unbranded calves who had partly attained their growth, were termed "mavericks," and when the herds of different owners mingled, there was, usually, a division of the mavericks, since it could not be accurately told who owned them.

The title maverick was derived from a stock man of that name, whose practice was to claim *all* unbranded calves in a herd. His cowboys would ride about, cutting out the unmarked animals, with the cool statement:

"That's a maverick," meaning that it belonged to their "boss."

And so the name has commonly become associated with any half-grown, unbranded calf.

Mr. Merkel was the owner of several ranches, Square M, Triangle B and Diamond X, not to mention Diamond X Second, or Flume Valley, of which his son Bud, and the latter's cousins, Norton and Richard Shannon, were the nominal proprietors.

The cattle from Flume Valley, or "Happy Valley" as Bud called it after the mystery of the underground water was solved, were in the round-up with the others from his father's ranches.

For days preceding the lively doings I have just described, the cowboys, called in from distant ranges, had driven the cattle toward the central assembling point - the corrals at Diamond X.

Slowly the longhorns, the shorthorns and cattle with no horns at all, had been "hazed" in from their feeding grounds toward Diamond X. The cow punchers had galloped hard all day, and they had ridden herd at night, to keep the animals from straying. At night this was not so hard, for the animals were glad to rest during the darkness.

But during the day there was always some steer - often more than one - that wanted to run away from the herd. As this might start a stampede it was necessary to drive the "striker" back, and this was, often enough, a difficult task.

Bud, Nort and Dick had borne their share of this difficult round-up task, and now, when the thousand or more of steers, calves and mavericks had been gathered at Diamond X, the work of tallying them, branding those that were without marks and shipping away the best was well under way.

In and out of the herd rode the boy ranchers, doing their best alongside of more seasoned "punchers." Calves were cut out, thrown and branded, to be quickly released and again mingle with the herd.

Willard F. Baker

"Oh, I'm Captain Jinks,
Of the Horse Marines!"

One of the cowboys, wiping the dust and sweat from his face, with his big, red silk handkerchief, or, rather, neckerchief, started this song. It was taken up by half a score of loud voices.

"Yi-yippy!" came in stentorian tones from Yellin' Kid. "This is the life!"

But as, just then, his pony slipped and he missed the throw he made for a calf, it is doubtful if Yellin' Kid felt as gay as he sounded.

"Hot work; eh, boys?" asked Mr. Merkel, when Dick, Nort and Bud rode past to get drinks of water.

"But it's great, all the same!" answered Dick, with shining eyes - eyes that gleamed amid a face dark with the tan of the western sun and grimy with the dust of the western plains.

"Glad you like it!" commented the proprietor of Diamond X as he kept on with his tallying. "How they coming, Slim?" he asked his foreman.

"Couldn't be better! Old Buck Tooth is doing a heap sight more than I ever dreamed a Zuni could."

"Bud said that his old Indian helper was up to snuff!" commented Mr. Merkel. "I'm glad to know it. Heard anything from Double Z?" he asked, and there was an anxious note in his voice.

"No, Hank and his gang seem to have quieted down

after what I told 'em!"

"Well, I hope he doesn't make trouble for Bud and the boys. They're going back to Happy Valley to-night."
"So I understand. Oh, shucks! Don't worry about Hank! He's all talk - he and that blustery foreman of his, Ike Johnson!"

There had been a dispute between the cowboys of Diamond X and those of Double Z, a ranch owned by the notorious Hank Fisher, a few days before the round-up, the subject of dispute being the ownership of certain mavericks. It had ended with the triumph of Slim Degnan, foreman of Mr. Merkel's holdings.

And so the round-up went on, the heat, the dust, the noise and confusion increasing as calf after calf, maverick after maverick, was branded, and the steers to be shipped were cut out, to be hazed over to the railroad stock yards.

And yet, with all the seeming confusion, there was order and system in the work.

"Well, I guess this is the last," remarked Mr. Merkel to his son, as Bud, with his cousins, rode slowly up to the ranch house, when the final calf had been cut out and the tally made. "You boys going back after grub?"

"Yep," answered Bud, but there was no enthusiasm in his voice. He, like his cousins, was too tired. For the day had been a grueling one, with the heat and hard work.

"You sure did make out a whole lot better than I ever thought you would," said Mr. Merkel, as he rode along with his son and nephew's. "Putting water into that valley made a big difference."

"I should say so!" exclaimed Bud. "Our stock will lay over anything you will ship from any of your three ranches, Dad!"

"I wouldn't wonder but what you are right, Bud! Well, let's wash up and eat."

One by one the cowboys drifted in, some singing ranch songs in spite of their weariness. Bud and his cousins were through with their meal first, and, having persuaded his sister, Nell, to pack a basket of dough-nuts, pie and cheese for him, Bud signalled to his cousins to join him out at the pony corral.

"Let's get an early start back to Happy Valley," he urged. "It's a long enough ride, anyhow."

"You said it!" commented Nort.

"Well, there's one thing we don't have to worry about, and that is not finding any water running into the reservoir," added Dick, as he slipped in through the gate and caught one of his ponies - not Blackie, who was tired out from the round-up. Each cow puncher, including the boy ranchers, had several animals in his "string."

"No, I guess, since we solved the mystery of the water supply, we'll have no more trouble," agreed Bud.

The boy ranchers rode over the trail to their own camp - it was actually a camp, for permanent ranch buildings had not yet been erected in Happy Valley, though some were projected. Tents formed the abiding place of our heroes, and as they were only there during the summer months the canvas shelters served very well, indeed.

The moon rose, shining down from a starlit sky, as the rough but faithful and sturdy cow ponies ambled along. Now the boy ranchers would be down in some swale, or valley, and again topping one of the foothills which led to Buffalo Ridge or Snake Mountain, between which elevations lay Happy Valley, where the cattle of Diamond X Second were quartered.

"There she is - the old camp," murmured Dick, as they started down the slope which led to the collection of tents erected against the earthen and stone bank of the reservoir.

"And maybe I won't hit the hay!" exclaimed Bud, with a yawn. "We don't have to get up to-morrow until we're ready."

"Oh, boy!" cried Nort in delight.

They rode forward, and were almost at their camp when Bud, who had trotted ahead, pulled his pony to a sudden stop and cried out:

"Hold on there! Who are you and where are you going?"

At the same moment his cousins saw the moon gleaming on the .45 gun which Bud drew from his holster.

CHAPTER II

A CURIOUS INSTRUMENT

"What's the matter, Bud?" asked Dick, as he urged his animal forward in a jump, until he was beside his cousin,

"Some one's up there around the tunnel entrance," responded Bud Merkel. "I saw 'em dodge back out of the light." Then, raising his voice, he cried: "Come on, now! None of your tricks! I've got you covered!"

"I don't see any one," spoke Nort.

"They're there, all right," asserted Bud. "Come on, fellows," he exclaimed, "we'll have to look into this. There was trouble enough with getting water to stay in Happy Valley, without letting some Greaser in to queer the works again! Come on!"

He and his cousins rode their horses up the rather steep and winding trail that led from the bottom of the reservoir to the top, where a big iron pipe, sticking out under the mountain like the head of some great serpent, brought from the distant Pocut River a stream, without which it would have been impossible to raise cattle in the valley the boy ranchers claimed as particularly their own.

"Who you reckon it is?" asked Nort, as his pony scrambled up between the animals of Dick and Bud.

"Oh, some prowler that may have been rustling our grub while we were over at the round-up," was the answer.

"They couldn't get any cattle, for there aren't any to get," observed Dick. This was true, as all the animals had been driven from Happy Valley over to Diamond X. Later such as were not shipped away, and many of the calves and mavericks would be returned to fatten up and grow in readiness for the spring tallying.

"I don't just like this!" murmured Bud, as he again urged his pony forward. "Have your guns ready, fellows!"

And while they are thus riding toward the place where a strange tunnel pierced Snake Mountain, I shall take this opportunity to present, more formally than I have yet had a chance to do, my new readers to the boy ranchers. For that is what Bud Merkel, and Nort and Dick Shannon called themselves, being that, in fact.

Bud was a western lad, the son of Henry Merkel, who had been a ranchman all his mature years. He lived at Diamond X ranch, with his wife and daughter Nell. Some time before this present story opens Bud's cousins from the east had come to spend the summer with him, while their father and his wife made a trip to South America.

Nort and Dick, though "tenderfeet" at the beginning, had quickly fallen into the ways of the west, and in the first volume of this series, "The Boy Ranchers," I was privileged to tell you how they helped solve a mystery that revolved around Diamond X.

This mystery had to do with two college professors, and a strange, ancient animal. But it would not be fair to my new readers to disclose, here, all the secrets of that book.

So successful was the first summer which Nort and Dick spent at their uncle's ranch, that they were allowed to repeat it the following season. But this time there was a change. As related in the second volume, "The Boy Ranchers in Camp," Mr. Merkel had, by utilizing an ancient underground water-course beneath Snake Mountain, and by making a dam in Pocut River, brought water to a distant valley he owned.

This valley was originally called Buffalo Wallow, the source of the name being obvious. But once water was brought through the underground course, and piped to a reservoir, whence it could be distributed to drinking troughs for the cattle, and also used to irrigate the land, it enabled a fine crop of fodder to be grown. With the bringing of the water to Buffalo Wallow, or Flume Valley, as Bud called the place, it was possible to do what had never been done before - raise cattle there. Bud's father let him take this valley ranch as his own, and Nort and Dick were boy partners associated with their western cousin, Mr. Shannon putting up part of the needed capital to make the start for his sons.

All would have gone well except for the mysterious stoppage of the flow of water, which stoppage, if continued, would mean disaster.

How the water fight at Diamond X Second (as the

valley ranch was sometimes called) ended, and how the strange mystery was solved, is the story in the second volume, and I absolutely refuse to go into more details about it here. It would not be playing the game square.

At any rate the water was finally turned back into the underground tunnel, and then, in order to better guard this vital necessity, Mr. Merkel had the entrance to the tunnel boarded up - egress being possible only when heavy doors, at either end, were unlocked.

I might say that while the tunnel was the old water-course of a vanished river, the shaft under the mountain appeared, in. ancient times, to have been used by the Aztecs, or some Mexican tribes, for hiding their store of gold away from the Spaniards. There were secret passages and rooms in the tunnel, to say nothing of hidden water gates.

Who had constructed these, and what actual use had been made of them was, of course, lost in the dim and ancient past. But that it was the Aztecs, or some allied race, was the statement of learned men who examined the tunnel.

After the water fight at Diamond X Second had terminated in favor of the boy ranchers, and great copper levers that operated the hidden water gates had been removed, the tunnel was boarded up, and was now seldom entered.

But now, as Bud and his cousins rode back from the big round-up, and the western lad had, as he thought, seen some one sneaking about the forbidden gate, there was a feeling of apprehension in the hearts of himself and cousins.

They had now reached the top level of the reservoir which held a storage supply of water. The reservoir was a great semi-circular bank of earth and atones, wide enough on top for two to ride abreast.

"I don't see any one," remarked Nort, straining his eyes to pierce the gloom and shadows into which the face of the tunnel and the locked gate were thrown by the moonlight and clouds.

"Nor I," added Dick.

"Well, I saw some one!" insisted Bud. "It was a man, as sure as snakes, and he seemed to be trying to open the big gate."

This gate was made of heavy bolted planks and was set on hinges in a jamb of other planks and boards that closed the reservoir end of the tunnel water-course. A similar barrier and big door was at the Pocut River end.

"Well, if he was here, he seems to be gone," observed Nort "Maybe it was a sheep herder, Bud."

"Well, if any of that gentry think they can drive their flock over here, and water their woolies at my expense, they're mistaken," declared Bud with emphasis. "Sheep men have to be, I reckon, but they're out of place in a cow country. Hello, there!" he called, loudly. "Come on out and show yourself!"

But there was no answer, and the only sound, aside from the creaking of the damp saddle leathers, was the splashing of water as it flowed from the big pipe and into the reservoir.

"Guess he lit out," observed Bud, thrusting his gun back into the holster.

"Or else you didn't see him," chuckled Nort. "Maybe your eyes are full of dust, same as mine are, from that round-up."

"Oh, I saw somebody all right!" declared Bud. "Might 'a' been one of Buck Tooth's Indian friends making a call, but -"

He suddenly ceased speaking and leaned over in his saddle to gaze earnestly at something on the ground. It was something that glittered and shone in the mystic moonlight as Nort and Dick could see. "What's that?" inquired the latter.

In answer Bud slipped from his saddle and picked up the object which the moonlight had revealed.

"What in the world is this?" asked the boy rancher, as he held up a curious instrument. "Is this the start of another mystery!"

CHAPTER III

STARTLING NEWS

Leaping from their saddles, Nort and Dick hurried to the side of their cousin, chum and partner in the ranch venture. Eagerly they looked over his shoulder while he examined the strange object he had picked up, almost at the very door leading into the mysterious tunnel.

The instrument - for such it seemed to be - consisted of a shiny, nickeled part, which was what had reflected the moonlight, thus attracting Bud's attention to it. In addition there were two flexible tubes, of soft rubber, joining into one where they met the shiny metal.

The two tubes each terminated in hard rubber ends, pierced with a tiny hole, and on the end of the single tube was a bright metal disk. The whole formed a strange object, picked up as it was from the ground, and especially when the boy ranchers feared they had some cause for alarm.

"What in the world is it?" asked Bud, as he dangled it in front of his cousins. "I never saw anything like it before. Wait! I have it! Yellin' Kid said he was going to send to Kansas City for a flute he could play on. This must be part of it! He dropped it here; though that couldn't 'a' been him sneaking around the tunnel. But this is Yellin' Kid's musical instrument all right! Oh, won't I rag him, though! I wonder which end you blow in?"

"That isn't a musical instrument!" declared Nort, taking it from Bud's hand.

"Not What is it then?" asked the western ranch lad.

"It's a stethoscope," declared Nort.

"Whew! x I didn't know Yellin' Kid could play one of *them*!" exclaimed Bud. "He must be more musical than any of us thought!"

"'Tisn't musical, I tell you!" cried Nort, half laughing. "This is a *stethoscope* - it's what a doctor listens to your lungs or heart with when you're sick."

"He never listened to mine!" boasted Bud, "at least not since I can remember, for I've never been sick."

"Well, I have," admitted Nort, "and so has Dick. You remember Dr. Thompson using one of these, don't you?" he asked his stout brother.

"Sure I do! And there's some other name for it besides plain stethoscope," declared Dick. "It's a long word - bi - di -"

"Binaural stethoscope! That's it!" broke in Nort. "I remember, now. I thought I'd never be able to say those words, but they come back to me now. Binaural stethoscope."

Willard F. Baker

"'Tisn't good to eat, or shoot with, is it!" asked Bud, as he again took the instrument and turned it over and over in his hands.

"Eat! Shoot!" laughed Nort. "No, I tell you it's to listen to your heart beats, or lungs. Binaural means, simply, that it's fixed so you can listen with both ears at the same time. And stethoscope comes from two Greek words, stethos, the breast, and skopen, to view. It means, literally, to view inside the chest, but of course the doctors who use the stethoscope don't really do that. They only listen through the ear pieces - these," and he held up the two rubber tubes ending in hard nipples, pierced with small holes.

"What's the other end for!" asked Bud, indicating the shiny disk of metal that dangled from the single tube.

"That's the part the doctor holds on your chest or over your heart," Dick answered. "Sometimes the doctor puts it to your back to listen to your breathing from that side."

"Well, who in the world would have a - a binaural stethoscope out here!" asked Bud. "Yon reckon Doc. Tunison dropped it!" he went on, referring to the local veterinarian. "Shucks no! Cow doctors don't use 'em, not that I ever heard of," declared Nort. "Though Doc. Tunison is up to date."

"He sure was in discovering that it was germs which caused the epidemic outbreak in our stock last year," remarked Bud.

"Yes, we got out of that mighty lucky," chimed in Dick. "What's become of Pocut Pete?" he asked, referring to a scoundrel of a cowboy.

"Oh, Del Pinzo and Hank Fisher had pull enough to get him out of jail, after he'd served only part of his term for infecting our stock," said Bud. He had reference to something which is explained in the volume immediately preceding this. Del Pinzo was a notorious Mexican half-breed who, more than once, had made trouble for the boy ranchers. Hank Fisher was the owner of Double Z ranch, adjoining that of Square M, one of Mr. Merkel's, and also adjoining Happy Valley. Pocut Pete was believed to be a tool of these two unscrupulous men, and Del Pinzo had at his command Several Greasers who slipped back and forth over the Mexican border, not far from which were located the holdings of Mr. Merkel and the boy ranchers.

"Well, this is a stethoscope all right," went on Nort, as Bud turned toward his pony, with the evident intention of mounting.

"And I'd give a lot to know what it's doing here, and who dropped it," spoke Bud. "Let's look around a little more. I'm not at all satisfied with this. I sure saw, some one here, and this proves it," and he stuffed the doctor's instrument into his pocket.

"It doesn't prove that the man you saw - or thought you just saw - sneaking around here dropped it," spoke Nort. "We've been away for a week, and it may have been dropped any day within that time."

"Yes," agreed Bud. "But who was monkeying around here as we rode back to camp? That's what I want to know!"

However, search as the boy ranchers did, they found no midnight visitor. All was quiet at their camp, save for the distant howl of a coyote, and the splash of the water into the reservoir. All the stock had been driven away from Happy Valley to the big round-up at Diamond X, but soon the fertile glade would again be dotted with hungry cattle.

"Well, I reckon we'll have to give up," said Bud, when a thorough search had been made, and no one discovered.

"The tunnel door doesn't show any signs of an attempt having been made to bust it; does it?" asked Dick.

"Not as far as I can see, in this light," Bud replied. "We'll take a stroll up here in the morning," he went on as he thrust the stethoscope into his pocket. "Now for a little grub, and then to hit the hay. Oh, boy! But I to tired!"

So were the others, and after rummaging among their camp stores, and eating some crackers and canned peaches, the boys, having picketed their horses, turned in, rolled up in their blankets, and were asleep almost as soon as their heads were on the pillows, which were, as a matter of fact, stuffed with hay.

An examination, next morning, disclosed nothing more in the neighborhood of the tunnel entrance than their own and, their ponies' feet marks, until Bud, with an exclamation, pointed to several cigarette stubs on the ground, and a number of half-burned matches.

"Some one was here last night - or yesterday!" he declared. "And they stood in this one spot for some time - either resting or spying."

"What would they be spying on!" asked Dick.

"Search me!" frankly admitted Bud. "But since we had that water fight I'm suspicious of everything. Those cigarette stubs are fresh, and were dropped last night, or yesterday. None of us use 'em, and though some of our cow punchers do they haven't been here lately enough to have left this fresh evidence. The stubs are new ones."

"Well, maybe there was some one here last night," said Dick.

"I'm positive of it!" declared Bud. "Let's take another look at the big door lock."

Even a close inspection, however, failed to disclose any signs of the great portal, or its heavy padlock having been tampered with. Nor were there any marks tending to show where an effort had been made to force boards off the frame in which the door was set.

"Well, we'll just have to wait," said Bud, as he turned to go back down to the tents. "Hello," he suddenly added, as he gazed off up the valley. "Here comes somebody, riding like all possessed, too!"

The boy ranchers watched the approach of the solitary horseman, and, as he drew nearer Bud exclaimed:

"It's Buck Tooth!"

It was, in fact, that same Zuni Indian, who had been engaged as a sort of camp cook and ranch hand by

Bud's father, later being transferred to Bud's service. Buck Tooth was devoted to the boy ranchers.

"What's matter, Buck! What for you ride so *pronto* fashion!" asked Bud as the Indian, a superb horseman, drew rein close to the boy ranchers. "You race, maybe, Buck Tooth!"

"Yep - race tell you bad news!" half - grunted the Zuni.

"Bad news!" faltered Bud. "Is it my mother - dad -"

"Them all well," said Buck Tooth. "But got bad news all same. You see anybody out here?" and he slipped from his saddle to rest his almost winded steed.

CHAPTER IV

THE SCRATCHED SAFE

Eagerly the boy ranchers gathered about Buck Tooth. The Indian, as if rather ashamed of the hurry and emotion that had possessed him, grew quieter as he threw the reins down over his pony's head, as an intimation to the animal not to stray. Then the Zuni turned toward Bud and his cousins.

"This is the second time you gave me bad news, Buck," remarked the western lad. "Remember?"

"How?" asked the Indian sharply.

"I say this is the second time you've brought news of something bad. You were the first to tell me about the water stopping in the reservoir. And from then on we had some rousing times; didn't we, fellows?" asked Bud, turning to his chums.

"That's right!" assented Nort.

"But what's going on now?" Dick wanted to know.

"You said it!" exclaimed Bud. "I should let Buck Tooth tell it, instead of keeping him gassing away about the past. What's the row, Buck?"

Willard F. Baker

"Robbers!" was the Indian's answer.

"Robbers? At Diamond X?" cried Bud.

"Did they get anything?" Dick wanted to know.

"Anybody hurt?" asked Nort.

"Get some money - nobody hurt only Babe - him get broken leg," half-grunted the Indian.

"Babe has a broken leg in a fight with robbers?" gasped Bud. "Shoot it along a little faster, Buck! I'm sorry I didn't let you ride harder at first. How much did they get? Was it rustlers, and I'll bet a cookie with a raisin in that Del Pinzo and his gang had a hand in the fracas! Did Babe shoot any of 'em?"

"Babe him try - but too fat," said the Indian, with as near to a chuckle as ever he achieved, "Fall down - bust leg. Your *padre* no can tell how much money gone, but big iron box not opened."

"Oh, they didn't get to the safe, then!" exclaimed Bud with relief in his voice. For he knew, at this season of the spring round-up, that many thousands of dollars, from the sale of cattle, were often kept in his father's safe. "But go ahead, Buck! Tell us more about it. Step on her! Give her the gas! Open the throttle!"

"Hu?" grunted the Zuni, questioningly. "I step on somet'ing?" "You're only mixing him up!" declared Nort "Let him take his own time, Bud."

"If I do he'll be until noon giving us the facts. And if the robbers looted dad's office, even if they didn't get the safe open, they may have lit out with a tidy sum, and we ought to take the trail after 'em. That's what Buck came here for, likely! To get us on the chase from this end. Go ahead! Shoot!" he requested, meaning a verbal fire, not actual.

Whether Buck Tooth would have succeeded, under these confusing directions, in making a quick, dear statement of the matter is a question that was not settled. For, just as the Indian was about to resume, Dick looked off toward the distant hills, which lined the trail between Diamond X proper, and Happy Valley, and the lad exclaimed:

"Here comes one of the robbers now, riding like Sam Hill!"

Bud and Nort leaped to the side of their partner, their hands on their weapons, but, after a glimpse of the approaching horseman, having shaded his eyes with his hands, Bud cried:

"That isn't a robber! It's Yellin' Kid. I know his riding. I reckon he's come to give us the straight of it!"

Which proved to be the case.

"Buck outrode me," admitted Yellin' Kid as he drew rein, and his voice was not as loud as usual. "We started at th' same time, shortly after midnight when th' break was made, but that Indian's cayuse shore can step some! An' Buck can ride - let me tell you!"

"You shot a ringer that time!" asserted Bud. "But what happened! And is Babe badly hurt!"

"No! He just twisted his ankle gettin' out of his bunk in a hurry t' take a pot shot at th' bunch that tried to hold us up. Doc. Tunison says he'll be all right in a week."

"But Tunison is a horse doctor!" objected Bud, for Babe, the fat assistant foreman of Diamond X, was a prime favorite with him and his cousins.

"Yes, shore he is! Why not? A horse doctor for a cow puncher!" chuckled Yellin' Kid. "But here's the yarn."

Thereupon, having turned his pony out to graze with the Indian's, Yellin' Kid told the boys what had happened.

"We started some of the cattle from th' round-up brandin' over to th' railroad," the cowboy stated, "an' followin' th' usual preliminaries we all settled down for th' night, after you fellows rode off. An' let me tell you I was glad t' hit my bunk!

"Well, some time near midnight we, out in th' bunkhouse, was roused up by shootin' from your father's bungalow, Bud. Course that couldn't mean but one thing, an' we all got our guns an' rushed out, natcherally. But all we saw was a bunch ridin' off in th' darkness, your father firin' at 'em, Bud.

"Come t' find out, your mother had been woke up by a noise in th' office where th' safe was. She called your father an' he took a look, with his gun, of course. He saw a man in a mask tryin' t' open th' strong box, and your dad gave th' usual countersign.

"But th' burglar wheeled, an' popped one at your dad, not hittin' him I'm glad t' say, an' out th' winder he jumped, th' burglar, I mean. Then the rest of th' gang, which was waitin', rode off, shootin' some, as your dad was doin'.

"Come t' find out, they'd got a few hundred dollars from the desk where your dad left th' cash, Bud, but th' main part was in th' safe, an' *that* they couldn't get open. Course soon as we knowed what was up we organized a posse, an' started off - all but Babe. He fell - or rolled - out of his bunk an' twisted his leg, somehow.

"Anyhow, Buck an' I was told off t' ride this way, partly t' let you fellers know what had happened, an' partly t' see if there was any trace of th' skunks what robbed your dad down here in Happy Valley. How about it? Seen anybody?"

"Well, yes, we did see some one sneaking around here when we arrived last evening," Bud answered. "But that was long before the robbery."

"And tell him what we found!" urged Dick

"Oh, yes, a stethoscope," went on Bud. "But that has nothing to do with the matter. Maybe some doctor, or medical student, is out here for his health, and dropped it as he rode over our place."

"What's a slitherscope!" asked Yellin' Kid. "Anything like a Triceratops?"

"No!" laughed Nort. "We'll show you. But say, what can we do toward getting these robbers?"

"We've got t' trail 'em," spoke the older cowboy, as he

turned to go to the tents with the boy ranchers, Buck Tooth following with the two half-winded ponies. "Soon as I get my breath - "

"That's right!" interrupted Bud. "Come on up and sit down. I'll make you some coffee. I forgot you'd ridden all night."

"Half of it, anyhow," asserted Yellin' Kid. "An' I rode hard! But so did Buck Tooth, only you'd hardly know it. He sure can make his cayuse cover th' ground!"

Indeed the Indian showed little signs of the hard riding he had accomplished between midnight and dawn. And when he and Yellin' Kid were having a belated morning cup of coffee further details of the story were told.

Who the robbers were, and how many there were in the gang that attempted to force the safe at Diamond X, were matters left to further enlightenment. Mr. Merkel had only seen one in his office, bending over the safe, and this one had fled at the command of "hands up!" Then the others had raced away, amid a fusillade of shots which they returned.

It was so dark - the moon of the early night having been clouded over - that the direction taken by the robbers had not been ascertained.

"They probably scattered," declared Yellin' Kid. "It would be th' safest way - for them! But there's a chance some might 'a' come this way, so your dad wanted you t' be on the watch."

"We will!" declared Bud. "And when some of the boys

come back on the job here, and we get our allotment of cattle so things settle down to normal, I'm going back to the ranch and have a talk with dad."

"'Twouldn't be a bad idea," agreed Yellin' Kid. "But where's that mouth organ you said you found?"

"A stethoscope," laughed Bud. "Here it is," and he exhibited the medical instrument.

"Hum!" mused the cowboy. "It might be a burglar tool for all I'd know the difference. But now, if it's agreeable t' you fellers, let's have a look around. Maybe some of them burglars got a chunk of lead in him and he's hidin' out around here."

However, a search in the vicinity of Happy Valley camp disclosed nothing, and then Bud and his cousins set about getting back into the routine that had been interrupted by the round-up.

"The first thing we've got to do," Bud declared, "is to mend that break in the telephone line. If that had been working last night you could have called us up, Kid, instead of you and Buck having to ride out here."

"Yes, we wished th' line was working" admitted the cowboy. "But it wouldn't have been of much use, it seems. Them burglars didn't come out this way. However, it's just as well t' have it fixed."

There was a system of telephones connecting Bud's camp with his father's main ranch and also the two branch ones, and the system was likewise hooked-up with the long distance. But a recent wind, just before the round-up, had blown down some poles in Happy

Willard F. Baker

Valley, putting Bud's line out of commission. This was why he and his chums could not be reached by wire from Diamond X.

The poles were set up in the next few days, when some cowboys arrived to again take up their duties with Bud, Nort and Dick; for the cattle not sold were again sent back to the valley range to fatten for the fall, and they needed to be looked after.

Meanwhile, a search of the surrounding country had failed to disclose any trace of the robbers, and their identity remained hidden. They had gotten away with about $500, missing a much larger sum in the safe. The authorities were notified, and a posse scoured the region, but fruitlessly.

"Let's have a look at the safe they tried to open, Dad," begged Bud, when he and his cousins had ridden over to pay a week-end visit to the home ranch. "Did they try to drill it for an explosive?"

"I don't believe so, son. In fact, I haven't looked at the safe very closely, except to notice that it was all right. And I took the money out of it over to the bank next day."

Bud and his cousins looked at the strong box in which Mr. Merkel kept his money and valuable papers. It was a large, old-fashioned safe, proof from any fire that might visit the ranch, and beyond the ability of ordinary burglars to open, without the use of explosives or special tools.

And as Bud leaned over to look at the heavy door he saw something that caused him to ask:

"Were these here before the attempted robbery, Dad?"

"What there, Bud?"

"These scratches on the front of the door. It does look as if they tried to drill the safe!"

Bud pointed to several parallel marks on the steel door. The scratches were deep in the paint, and seemed to radiate toward the shiny nickel dial of the combination. "Scratches!" repeated Mr. Merkel, coming over to look. "No, I never noticed them before. Why, she is clawed up some," he admitted. "But I can't say that they haven't been there since I got the safe, which was just before the round-up. Yes, she sure is clawed up some," and he spoke as if some mountain lion had done the damage to his strong box.

But here Bud's sister, Nell, took a hand in the proceedings.

"Those scratches are new ones - they were made by the burglar," declared the girl, whom Nort and Dick thought the prettiest they had ever seen. "I know, for I dusted your office, Dad, the day the round-up ended, and the door was as shiny then as a new penny."

"Then the burglar did it," decided Bud. "And it shows we have to deal with a regular gang of safe robbers, instead of just ordinary cattle rustlers!"

Willard F. Baker

CHAPTER V

THE BROKEN BOTTLE

Bud's opinion, expressed with such conviction, coupled with the fact that Nell, his sister, was sure the safe had not been scratched the day before the robbery, made it look as though men practiced in the evil art of burglary had been at work.

"When I saw the fellow, bending over my safe," said Mr. Merkel, "it appeared to me he was only trying to work the combination. I have a hard job, myself, remembering how to do it, account of the safe being a new one. And I was so surprised, at first, that I just stood there, like a locoed steer, watching him. Then I let out a yell, told him to throw his hands up, and things began to happen."

"But, instead of just trying to open your safe, by working the combination, same as I've heard of burglars doing by filing down their fingers with sandpaper to make 'em sensitive, he was getting ready to blow it open," declared Bud.

"Does look so. She sure is clawed!" commented Mr. Merkel again.

"Mercy! It's a wonder we weren't all blown up in our

sleep!" exclaimed Bud's mother. "You boys'll stay to dinner," she added, as if glad to change the subject.

"We aimed to," said Bud with a grin at his cousins. "We manage pretty well most times, with what we cook, and what Buck Tooth hands out in the grub line. But we sure do like a home-feed once in a while."

"Or twice!" added Nort, while Dick nodded his agreement.

But though it was evident that some professional burglar had endeavored to open the Merkel safe, that was all the conclusion which could be arrived at. No additional clues were found and, for a time, matters settled down into the ordinary run at Diamond X.

Summer was coming, with its heat, and Bud was glad there would be no interruption in the water supply that flowed into Happy Valley from the Pocut River, coming through the ancient underground passage.

"For we'll need plenty of water in hot weather," he told Jus cousins.

At Diamond X Second, as the outfit of the boy ranchers was often called, was now a goodly herd of animals eating the rich, Johnson grass and other fodder, getting fattened in readiness for sale in the fall, when there would be another round-up.

Besides Bud, Nort and Dick, there was now, at the camp in the valley, Buck Tooth the Zuni Indian, Yellin' Kid and Snake Purdee, two efficient and veteran cow punchers who had been transferred from Diamond X First, meaning by that the main ranch.

While Bud was a true son of the west, and while Nort and Dick had, some time ago, passed out of the tenderfoot class, still Mr. Merkel felt that his son and his nephews needed the aid and guidance of cattlemen older than themselves. So the "outfit," as the aggregation at a ranch is called, was quite a happy family.

"If we could only catch those burglars, and get back your dad's money, I'd feel better, though," declared Snake Purdee, as he rode in from the Diamond X ranch one day, to announce, among other news items, that Babe, the fat assistant foreman, was able to be about again.

"Yes," agreed Bud. "It isn't so much the money loss, as it is the knowledge that such a bunch of men is loose in a neighborhood. Del Pinzo and that Hank Fisher bunch are bad enough, but I don't believe they had a hand in this."

"I wouldn't put it past them!" stated Yellin' Kid in his usual, loud tones. "Th' skunks!"

"But dad said he didn't recognize the fellow he surprised at his safe," spoke Bud. "Of course he didn't have much chance. But if it had been Del Pinzo -"

"Don't worry!" broke in Snake Purdee. "That Greaser wouldn't do a job like that himself; or Hank Fisher, either. They'd get some one else to take the risk. However, what's th' use gassin' about it? I guess the money's gone for good. But I'm glad they didn't get th' safe open!"

"So'm I," chimed in Bud. "Some of our cash would

have vanished then." For he and his cousins had a share in the money received from the sale of steers at round-up time.

So, following the robbery at Diamond X, matters quieted down. Bud still kept the stethoscope, and word of the finding of the strange instrument traveled to other ranches. It was called by such a variety of names (the cowboys having twisted the original and proper one) until the boy ranchers had difficulty, at times, in understanding the reference when they were asked about it.

But no one claimed it, and no trace was found of the person who, it was presumed, had dropped it the night our heroes saw some one disappear near the boarded-up entrance to the ancient tunnel.

"Come on, let's try a bit of shooting!" proposed Nort one evening, when grub had been served at the camp, and he and his brother were left with Buck Tooth. Snake and Yellin' Kid had ridden off on an all-night tour of duty, to a, distant part of the ranch. A choice bunch of steers had started to wander farther off than Bud thought it was wise to let them. They were, evidently, in search of another variety of fodder, but that could not save them from some passing band of Greasers, or other cattle thieves.

"Haze 'em back this way," Bud had requested his two cowboys. "They'll be safer over here."

So Yellin' Kid and Snake had ridden away as the early evening shadows were falling and, to pass the time until the hour for seeking their bunks, the boy ranchers sought some amusement. Shooting at a mark was one form, and Nort and Dick were endeavoring to become as expert as their western cousin in the use of the .45.

"Shooting suits me," agreed Bud. "I'll soon have to cut down my handicap if you fellows keep on the way you're going," for in the tests of skill Bud had always discounted his own ability in order to be fair.

"Well, don't scale it down too much," begged Dick. "Nort hasn't got me skinned, but I'm not up to you."

"Well, let's see how you'll do," suggested Bud.

As a mark a bottle was stuck on a stick which was thrust into the ground at the foot of the sloping bank which enclosed the reservoir. Shooting against this earthen bank insured that no wild bullets would injure any one.

"You go first, Bud," suggested Dick. "We want to get a line on you."

Accordingly Bud walked to the marked-off place, drew his heavy revolver, raised it and brought it down on the mark - the bottle on the stick. There was a sharp crack, followed instantly by the tinkle of glass, and that bottle was no more.

"Busted it clean!" cried Nort. "I wish I could do that!"

Another flask was provided, and Nort shot at this. His aim was fairly good, but he was allowed to go five feet nearer than Bud had stood, that distance being the western lad's handicap. But Nort only chipped away part of the bottom of the bottle with his first shot, and it took three to shatter it completely,

"Watch me do better than that!" cried Dick, as he took his place where his brother had stood, and raised his gun. "I'll crack it first shot!"

His weapon was still in the air, and he had not brought it to a level with the bottle when there sounded, from somewhere out in the valley back of where the boy ranchers stood, the sound of a shot.

The bullet zipped viciously over their heads, and, as they instinctively ducked, they heard the crash of the broken bottle.

CHAPTER VI

MISSING STEERS

Like a flash Bud, who had been standing beside Nort, to watch the effect of Dick's try, turned and faced outward to view the darkening valley, whence had come the sound of that shot. Nort turned also, but Dick seemed to think one of his companions had played a trick on him.

"That isn't fair!" cried the stout lad. "What'd you want to go and bust that bottle for, Nort?"

"I didn't do it!" asserted his brother.

"Nor I," added Bud in a low voice. "The shot came from out there," and he indicated the long and fertile valley, over which the purple evening shadows were falling. "Duck, fellows!" he suddenly cried, and he pulled Nort beside him in the grass.

Dick, who caught the words of warning, and saw what his cousin had done, also dropped down, so that, a second or two after the firing of the strange shot that had shattered the bottle, only the heads of the boy ranchers showed above the grass, and then only slightly. "What's the idea?" asked Dick, as silence followed the measure of safety.

"Whoever it was that fired might shoot again," replied End.

"Who was it?" asked Nort.

"That's what we've got to find out," answered Bud in a low voice.

"Could it have been either Snake or Yellin' Kid, riding back and breaking that bottle over our heads, to show what good shots they were?" asked Dick.

"No, I hardly think so," replied his cousin. "They're both good shots, all right, and they could have broken that flask from the distance it was broken. But they wouldn't throw a scare into us this way. Besides, they haven't any time to fool around. They have an all-night ride ahead of them."

"What makes you think the bottle was busted from some distance, Bud!" Dick wanted to know.

"The way the bullet sounded," was the answer. "It was almost spent when it got here, but it had force enough to break the glass, and would have damaged us if it hit us. I thought whoever played that fool trick might try another shot, so I yanked you down, Nort."

"Glad you did! I might not have thought of it. But whoever it was doesn't seem to be going to shoot again."

"No," agreed Bud, after a little period of silence, during which no other menacing crack of a weapon was heard. "But we'll wait a little longer."

Through the fast-gathering darkness the boys looked out from their semi-hiding places across the valley. No wisp of smoke, and no movement of horse or rider was to be observed. And silence once more settled down on Happy Valley - not quite so happy as it had been. For, following the clearing-up of the mystery of the water supply, new and sinister events seemed pending for the boy ranchers.

But, as yet, there were only straws, showing which way the evil wind was blowing.

"Could it have been a chance shot?" asked Dick, raising himself a little to get a better look.

"That bullet was aimed straight for the bottle, over our heads," declared Bud. "It was no chance shot."

"One of ours couldn't have glanced, could it?" Dick wanted to know.

"Surely not!" affirmed Bud. "Why, no one had shot for some time. I'd just put the new bottle on the stick for you."

"Yes, and I was just going to shoot, when somebody took the bullet out of my gun, so to speak," went on Dick, grimly jesting.

"Do you think they were shooting at - us?" asked Nort, hesitatingly.

Bud did not answer for the moment, and when he did it was to say, as he suddenly arose:

"If they did I'm going to give 'em another chance. And

I'm going to do some shooting on my own account!" He had his gun in his hand, for he had so held it since he had shattered the first bottle, and now it was grasped in readiness for instant action.

"We're with you!" cried Nort and Dick, as they emerged from their recumbent positions in the grass, and hastened to the side of their cousin.

But though they looked across the valley, now half shrouded in gloom, and up and down, as far as they could see, no one was in sight. Here and there were small herds of their cattle. Back at the camp tents Buck Tooth was performing his evening duties, or "chores," as Bud called them. The Indian paid no attention to the shooting, for he knew the boys had gone to practice, and he could not be expected to realize that one of the shots was, possibly, a hostile one.

I use the word "possibly" with reason, for, as yet, there was nothing to show that it was not either an accident, or had not been fired by some passing cowboy who, from a distance, seeing the bottle on a stick, could not resist a chance to "take a crack" at it. And yet this last theory would seem to be a poor one. For if the shot had been a joke the one who had fired it would, in all reason, it appeared, have shown himself soon after.

"No one seems to show up," remarked Nort at length, in a low voice.

"Then we'd better look for 'em before it gets too dark," declared Bud. "Come on! Let's get our horses."

"Isn't it taking a chance, riding out to look for some one who may have fired at us purposely?" asked Dick.

"Yes," agreed Bud, after a moment's thought, "but life out west is all more or less of a chance and risk. You take a risk, every time you ride at more than a foot-pace, of your pony stepping into some prairie dog's hole and not only laming himself, but killing you. But you don't stop riding on that account."

"No," agreed Nort.

"And we take a chance every time we ride herd," went on Bud. "The steers may stampede, and before we can get 'em to milling, they may rush over us. But I notice neither of you ever back out of that job; do you?"

"No," agreed Nort, adding: "Well, then, I reckon going after this unknown shooter isn't taking such a long chance."

"I'm with you!" exclaimed Dick.

Briefly telling Buck Tooth what had happened, the boy ranchers rode off at a fast pace, to take advantage of what little light of day remained. They headed, as nearly as they could ascertain it, in the direction whence the single shot had come. But it is hardly need-less to say they found no one, and no sign that could be construed into a tangible clue.

"We'll tell Snake and Yellin' Kid about it when they come back," decided Bud, as he and his cousins returned to camp when darkness had completely fallen. For it was useless, after that, to search for the perpet-rator of the joke.

Or was it a joke?

That is what the boy ranchers asked themselves more than once.

Contrary to their half-formed expectations, the night passed quietly. There was no disturbance among the cattle, and no midnight visitors invaded the camp. But, for all this, the slumbers of our heroes were not easy. Perhaps they had premonitions of coming disaster.

For disaster came, with the return, early on the morning of the next day, of Snake and Yellin' Kid.

"They're after you, Bud!" shouted the cowboy with the loud voice. "They're after you!"

"Who?" asked Bud, as he and his cousins came out to meet the cowboys.

"Rustlers!" was the grim answer. "There's a lot of your steers missin' from that far herd! Rustlers, Bud! Rustlers!"

Willard F. Baker

CHAPTER VII

FOUR EYES

For a moment Bud Merkel seemed unable to comprehend the bad news thus brought to him by his cowboy helpers and friends. Nort and Dick, also, were shocked by the intelligence. But Bud quickly recovered. Perhaps it was because of his heritage of the west - the ability to face danger and disaster with grim courage, part of his father's stock in trade.

"Rustlers, eh?" repeated Bud, and his voice was steadier than Yellin' Kid or Snake Purdee expected to find it. "Did they get many?"

"Quite a bunch," answered Yellin' Bad. "We rounded up as many as we could, and -"

"You mean you rounded up the *rustlers*?" asked Nort, eagerly.

"No, what was left of the steers," answered Snake. "Guess we wouldn't be back here alone - that is, just us two, if we'd had a run-in with the rascals. We didn't see 'em, but we did find traces of 'em. What are you going to do, Bud? Get on their trail?"

"Let's talk it over, first," suggested the boy rancher,

and he looked at Nort and Dick, for they were partners with him on this venture of trying to raise cattle in Happy Valley - which would have been almost a desert save for the water that came through the strange mountain tunnel.

"Tell us about it," urged Dick.

"Well, there isn't so much to tell," replied Yellin' Kid, his voice a bit lower, now that there was serious business afoot. "Snake an' I started there, to haze back th' steers as you; told us, Bud. But when we'd rounded up th' herd, drivin' 'em in from where a lot of 'em had strayed, we saw, right away, that th' count was short. First we thought a bunch was hidin' out on us, but we made a pretty good search an' then we got th' evidence."

"The evidence?" exclaimed Nort.

"Yes, we saw where the rustlers had been at work. They must 'a' been there a day before we arrived. They probably cut out a good bunch of cattle an' drove 'em off. But they didn't drive 'em all."

"What makes you think so?" asked Bud. "Do you mean that we have a few left?" and he laughed uneasily.

"Oh, there's more'n a *few*," said Snake. "But by evidence Kid means we saw where they'd been blurrin' the brand - the Diamond X brand!"

"Oh, they're doing that; are they?" asked Bud, sharply.

"Yes, we found th' ashes of two or three brandin' fires," went on Yellin' Kid, "an' we picked up th' broken handle of a brandin' iron. No marks on it, like there was on the other," he said, referring to the time one of the irons from Double Z had been found on the range of the boy ranchers. "But we brought it along, anyhow," and he exhibited a broken and charred piece of wood.

"But we found more than that," he continued. "We found one steer they'd killed, for beef likely, after they'd blurred th' brand. There wasn't much left. What th' rustlers didn't take th' buzzards did. But there was enough of th' hide left to show what work they were up to - blurring th' brand."

This, as you have learned from the previous books of this series, consists in burning some other mark over the legitimate brand on cattle, so that the original one can not be made out. Then the animal may be claimed by whoever has it. Blurring a brand, that is, making it illegible, or changing one brand into another, are two of the methods used by unscrupulous men to steal cattle.

The boy ranchers well understood what was meant by the news brought them by the two cowboys. The next thing to decide on was what course to pursue. "Did they leave any trail?" asked Bud.

"Well, we didn't stop t' hunt for it, as long as it wasn't a plain one," Snake answered. "Likely we could 'a' picked it up. But as long as there had been a raid we decided th' best thing t' do was t' save th' rest of th' cattle, an' then come an' tell you, Bud."

"How many cattle do you think they took?" asked Nort.

"Oh, I should say fifty," answered Yellin Kid, "includin' th' one they killed for beef. Probably they blurred th' brands on th' others an' drove 'em off - an' I shouldn't be a bit s'prised," he went on, "but what we'd find most of your cattle, Bud, walkin' around on Double Z."

"Hank Fisher; eh?" exclaimed Dick.

"Yes, an' that slick Mexican half-breed of his, Del Pinzo!" declared Snake. "Anyhow, they got away with a bunch of your steers, Bud, an' now what are we goin' t' do? Are we goin' t' sit back an' let 'em laugh at us?"

"Not much!" declared the boy rancher. "But let's get this straight. I wonder why they didn't drive off the whole herd while they were at it?"

"Probably it was too big a contract for 'em," remarked Yellin' Kid. "An' then, too, they might not 'a' had men enough, or th' cattle may 'a' stampeded."

"An' maybe they was scared off," added Snake.

"Yes," agreed his partner on the ride from which they had just returned, "that may have been so. Somethin' may have scared th' rustlers. But if I get a chance at 'em, I'll throw a bigger scare int' 'em!" and he significantly tapped the grim .45 at his hip.

"Any trace of which way they went?" asked Bud.

"There is - up to a certain point," admitted Snake.

"What do you mean?" the boy rancher asked.

"Well, I mean we could trace the cattle down the valley up to that low place between the hills-a sort of pass. And then all trace of 'em was lost."

"Lost!" repeated Nort.

"Yes, sir, lost!" declared Snake. "You couldn't see any more signs of 'em than if they'd been lifted up in one of them flying machines and histed up over the mountain! That's th' funny part of this raid."

"There have been some other queer things around here," said Dick. "There was that bottle last night."

"What was that?" asked Snake, quickly.

"There was some promiscuous shooting around here last night," said Bud. "I'll tell you about it as soon as we get the straight of this rustler business. Maybe there's some connection. But I wonder -"

He was interrupted by a voice singing, and the song was one of the usual cowboy refrains, though the voice was rather better than usual.

At first the boy ranchers thought it might be Old Billee Dobb who, with Buck Tooth, had been out to a distant part of the valley to see if he could get on the track of a mountain lion which had been killing cattle. But a glance showed the approaching singer, who was also a rider, to be a stranger. He sat astride a big, black horse, much larger than the ordinary cow pony, and as he approached the camp the sun glinted in curious fashion on his face.

"Four eyes!" exclaimed Snake, meaning, thereby, that

the stranger wore glasses. The rising sun had reflected on their lens. On came "Four Eyes," singing as he advanced, until, when he came within hailing distance, he drew rein, saluted the assembled company with a half-military gesture and called out:

"Any chance of a job here?"

CHAPTER VIII

THROWING THE ROPE

Silence followed this greeting and question, and then the two boy ranchers, and their cowboy friends, waited for Bud to speak, he being, in a sense, the head of the new organization. Though Dick and Nort held equal shares, purchased for them by their father, the two lads who had lived so long in the east deferred to the boy of the west in this matter, thinking, naturally, that he would better be able to handle it.

"Looking for a place?" asked Bud, genially enough, as he surveyed the newcomer, from the top of his broad-brimmed range hat to the pawing hoofs of his black steed, for the horse was impatiently digging in the dirt.

"Yep!" was the answer. "I'm looking for a place." The voice was pleasant, and there was none of that clipping off of the final "g" in his words, so common a practice among most of the cowboys. Perhaps they didn't have time to use the proper endings. "I'm dead anxious to ride for some outfit," went on "Four Eyes," as he had been dubbed and as he came to be called, as long as he remained with Diamond X Second. "Your father sent me over here," he added.

"My father!" exclaimed Bud. "Do you know him? I

don't know you!" he added quickly, for he sensed that the stranger, in some manner, had managed to pick him from all the others as the son of the proprietor of Diamond X.

"I don't claim to know your father, only having met him once, when I rode up, yesterday, to ask for a job," went on Four Eyes. "I slept out last night - back there," he added with a wave of 'is quirt in the direction of Diamond X. "Had supper with the boys at your father's ranch, and he told me you might be needing some one. If you don't -" He paused suggestively, evidently ready to ride on and try his luck elsewhere if there was no chance in the valley.

"I may need some one," Bud said. In fact, he was in need of an additional hand, and since this latest action on the part of rustlers he wanted help more than ever, for he was about to put into execution a plan for getting on the trail of these marauders. "But how'd you know who I was?" he asked, anxious to ascertain how the stranger had picked him out, as distinguished from Nort or Dick.

"Oh, your father looks like you," was the easy answer, given with a laugh, in which Snake, Yellin' Kid and the boy ranchers joined. "When he said he didn't need any riders, adding that perhaps you might, I decided to take a chance."

"All right. I can use another hand - or, rather, *we* can," and Bud waved his hand toward his cousins. "You can turn your pony into the corral," he added, "and we'll give you something to eat - unless you've had breakfast?" he questioned.

"Not so much but what I can eat more. Thanks! My name's Henry Mellon. I've ridden some for Curly Q and Long L if you want any references."

"I reckon my dad sized you up all right," spoke Bud.

"I reckon he did!" laughed Henry Mellon, or Four Eyes, as I shall call him, following the custom of the others on the ranch. "I wouldn't want to try to put anything over on him."

"It isn't exactly healthy," agreed Bud, for his father bore an enviable reputation for finding out the truth about matters in that "cow country."

"Ever ride for Double Z?" asked Yellin' Kid, and the loud tone's of his voice appeared to startle the newcomer.

"Why, no," was the answer. "I can't say that I have. One of Mr. Merkel's ranches?" he asked.

"No. It's Hank Fisher's place," spoke Snake. "Glad to meet up with you," he added, riding forward and extending his hand. "That's quite a hoss you got there. Beckon he can go some!"

"Well, he doesn't take dust from many," was the cautious admission, as the new cowboy shook hands all around. "He'll be glad of a rest, though, for I've ridden hard lately. I suppose I can use another?" he asked Bud.

"Sure," was the answer. "Snake here, or Yellin' Kid, will show you which ones you can add to your string. See you later, fellows," Bud called to his cowboy helpers, as he motioned to Nort and Dick to follow him to their own private tent.

"What do you think of it, Bud?" asked Nort, when they were alone, and the new cowboy was being made to feel at home by Snake, Yellin' Kid, and Old Billee, who had by this time ridden in. The smell of cooking arose from the tent that Buck Tooth had turned into a kitchen.

"You mean him?" and Bud nodded toward where the cowboys were congregated in friendly talk.

"No, I mean about the rustlers."

"Oh, they're bad! No question about it - they're *bad!*" declared Bud. "As soon as we get a chance we'll ride over and take a look at the place. It doesn't seem reasonable that they can drive a bunch of cattle off down the valley, and then have all traces of 'em disappear as if they'd gone up in an airship."

"That's right!" chimed in Dick. "Do you s'pose this Four Eyes saw the rustlers?"

"He didn't come from that direction," declared the western lad.

"He *says* he didn't," spoke Nort. And when Nort accented that one word Bud looked at his cousin quickly.

"Don't you believe what he says?" Bud asked.

"All the same I'd call up your father," went on Nort.

Willard F. Baker

Bud hesitated a moment and then said:

"I will! No use taking chances. He may be all right, but it won't do any harm to know it. I like his looks, though we don't often get a cowboy with glasses. I'll call dad!"

Which he did, on the telephone, learning from his father that Mr. Merkel knew nothing about the stranger, though he "sized him up," as being all right.

But Mr. Merkel had done more than this. He had called, on the telephone, or had been in communication, otherwise, with the late employers of Henry Mellon, and the cowboy was well spoken of. He was a reliable hand, it was said.

"So we don't have to worry about *him*," Bud told his cousins. "But we do have to take some action about these rustlers! Hang 'em! I wish they were all bottled up in the tunnel!"

"That's right!" chimed in Dick.

"Are we going on their trail?" asked Nort.

"If we can pick it up," agreed Bud. "Anyhow, we'll take a ride over that way. What with cattle missing, and queer shots being fired behind your back, we're likely to be in for as lively a time as when we had the water fight!"

"Or locating a Triceratops!" added Nort with a laugh.

After breakfast, and the finishing of the usual "chores" about camp, the boy ranchers prepared to ride over and look at the place where the raid had been made. "What cattle had not been taken - and it was only a small part of the herd that had been driven off - were now nearer the camp headquarters, having been hazed over by Snake and Yellin' Kid. Mr. Merkel had been told of the theft, and had advised prompt action on the part of his son and nephews.

"Four Eyes seems to be making himself right at home," remarked Dick, as the three boys started toward the corral, intending to saddle their ponies and ride over to the scene of the cattle-rustling operations.

"Yes," agreed Bud.

Henry Mellon was in the midst of Old Billee, Buck Tooth, Snake and Yellin' Kid, and, as the boy ranchers watched, they saw N Four Eyes twirling his lariat above his head.

"What's he doing?" asked Dick.

"Oh, just showing 'em some fancy roping," Bud answered.

"Let's go over," suggested Nort. "I'd like to get on to a few tricks, myself."

They found Four Eyes attempting some of the more difficult feats of rope throwing. After twirling his lasso about his head, the rope forming a perfect circle, he changed the direction from horizontal to perpendicular, and nimbly leaped backward and forward through the swiftly circling lariat.

Snake tried this, but his spurs caught and there was a

queer mix-up of man and rope. Snake could equal the newcomer's feat in twirling the rope around his head horizontally, but failed, as did Yellin' Kid, in the other trick.

"It's just a knack," said Four Eyes, modestly enough. "I had a lot of spare time, and I practiced some of these fancy twists. I can rope four horses at once."

"Yes you can - not!" challenged Snake.

"I'll prove it - of course they have to be going in the same direction," stipulated the new cowboy.

"Even with that I doubt it," went on Snake. "I've heard of that, but I never saw it done."

"If you fellows will ride past me I'll rope you all," and Four Eyes indicated Snake, Yellin' Kid, Old Billee and Buck Tooth. They mounted horses, and as Bud, Nort and Dick watched, the newcomer prepared for the test.

CHAPTER IX

THE FIRE

"Sat when!" called Snake to the spectacle-wearing cowboy, as the reptile-fearing cow puncher and his companions prepared to let themselves be roped by the new arrival - providing he could do it.

"I'll be ready in a moment," remarked Henry Mellon, and Bud and his cousins could not but note how differently he spoke from the average run of ranch hands.

"More like one of those college professors who were after the ten-million-year-old Triceratops," remarked Nort, commenting on the talk.

"Yes, he is a bit cultured in his speech," assented Bud. "Guess he hasn't been out west long."

"Then how can he be such a wonderful roper?" Dick wanted to know, for there was no doubt about the ability of Four Eyes, even if he had not yet made good oh his boast of putting his lariat around four galloping horses at once.

"Oh, well, it comes natural to some people," said Bud, "and then, too, he may have been in Mexico. Some of

Willard F. Baker

the Greasers are pretty slick with the horsehair. But let's watch."

By this time the four cow punchers, counting Buck Tooth as one, for the Indian was a good herdsman, had lined themselves up about a hundred feet from where Four Eyes sat on his horse - not the same black one he had ridden in, but another, of Bud's stock, that had been assigned him.

"Ready?" asked Yellin' Kid.

"All ready! Come a running!" shouted Four Eyes, and even here he did not drop a "g."

In an instant the four horses were in motion, coming together, in line, down the stretch which the newcomer faced. In another moment Four Eyes had ridden across the path of the oncoming steeds, and on the ground he spread out his lasso in a great loop, leaning over in his saddle to do this. He retained hold of the rope end that was fastened to his saddle, and then, having spread the net, as it were, he pulled up on the opposite side of the course down which the four were now thundering in a cloud of dust.

"Can he do it?" asked Nort.

"He can that way - yes," Bud said. "It's a trick! I thought he was going to make a throw."

"It's a good trick, though, if he does it," declared Dick.

In another instant all four horses ridden by the cowboys and the Indian were within the spread-out loop of Four Eyes as it lay on the ground. And then something happened.

With a mere twist of his wrist, as it seemed, Henry Mellon snapped the outspread rope upward and, reining back his horse, he suddenly pulled the lasso taut.

It was completely around the sixteen legs of the four horses, holding them together, the rope itself being half way down from the shoulder of each animal.

"He did it! By the great rattler and all the little rattlers, he did it!" shouted Yellin' Kid, as he pulled his horse to a stop, an example followed by the others. For though they might all (save one, perhaps) have pulled out of the encircling rope, there possibly would have been an accident. One, or more, of the horses would have stumbled, or been pulled to the ground. And there was no need of that in what was only a friendly contest.

"You did it!" declared Yellin' Kid, as Four Eyes loosed his rope and it fell to the ground, the riders guiding their horses out of the loop. "You shore did it!"

"But it was a trick!" declared Old Billee. "'Tw'an't straight ropin'!"

"Yes, it's a trick, but not every one can do it," said the new cowboy.

"Betcher I can!" declared Snake.

He tried - more than once, but failed. It was not as easy as it looked, in spite of the fact that it was a trick.

"No one can throw, with any accuracy, a loop big

enough to take in four horses on the run," declared Four Eyes when it had been demonstrated that he alone, of all the "bunch" at the Happy Valley ranch, could do what he had done. "At least if they can, I've never seen it. Two, maybe, or three, but not four. Putting your rope on the ground, and snapping it up as the horses get in it, is the only way I know."

"I wish you'd show me," spoke Nort.

"I will," promised Four Eyes. "You don't often have need for a trick like it, but it may come in useful some day."

Then he showed the boys the knack of it, though it was evident they were not going to master the "how" in a hurry.

Other feats in roping were indulged in by the cowboys, but none was as expert as Four Eyes. He seemed to possess uncanny skill with the lariat, though some of his tricks could be duplicated by Snake, Yellin' Kid and even by the boy ranchers.

But life on a western ranch is not all fun and jollity, though as much of this as possible is indulged in to make up for the strenuous times that are ever present. So, after the roping exhibition was over, and the newcomer had been assigned certain duties, Bud, Nort and Dick rode down the valley, intending to look over the place where the steers had been stolen, and the carcass of one left as a grim reminder of the raid.

Otherwise all in Happy Valley was peaceful. The water was running into the reservoir, through the pipes that connected with the mysterious underground course, once utilized, it was thought, by the ancient Aztecs.

Here and there, feeding on the rich bunch and Johnson grass, were the cattle in which the boy ranchers were so vitally interested. The most distant herd had been driven in by Snake and Yellin' Kid - the herd on which the raid had been made. Like black specks on the green floor of the valley were the cattle, dotted here and there.

"If we have luck this season we ought to round up a good bunch this fall," observed Bud, as he rode with his cousins.

"Yes," agreed Nort. "The water can't be shut off now, and we have nothing to worry about."

"Except rustlers," put in Dick.

"And the fellow who broke the bottle for us," added Bud. "I'd like to know who he was."

"It was a bit queer," Nort admitted. "But I believe it was some passing cow puncher playing a joke on us. This cattle stealing is no joke, though, and it's got to stop!"

"You let loose an earful that time," spoke Bud, in picturesque, western slang. "We'll have to let the bottle-breaker wait for a spell, until we size up this rustler question. We may have to get up a sheriff's posse and clean out the rascals."

"If we can find 'em," grimly added Dick.

It was some distance to the place where Yellin' Kid

and Snake Purdee had seen evidences of the raid, and it was long past noon when the boys reached it. They had stopped for "grub" on the way, having carried with them some food. Water they could get from one of the several concrete troughs that had been installed, the fluid coming through pipes from the reservoir.

"Here's where they killed the steer, or yearling," Bud said, pointing to a heap of bones.

It was all that remained from the feast of the buzzards.

"And here's where they started to drive off the cattle, evidently," added Nort, pointing to where a plain trail, made by the feet of many animals, led away from the ground that was more generally trampled by a large herd.

"Let's follow it," urged Dick. "We want to see when it gets to the disappearing point"

"That's right!" chimed in Bud.

They urged their ponies slowly along the trail left by the rustlers. It seemed to go down the valley to the place where the hills lowered on either side to form a sort of pass. It was in this pass that the two cowboys said the trail was lost.

"We've got some distance to go, yet," observed Bud, as they paused to look and make sure they had not lost the trail.

"And, after all, maybe we'll only find the same thing Snake and Kid did - nothing!" said Nort.

"Well," began Bud, "we've got to get to the bottom of this, and if we don't in one way we will -"

He was interrupted by a shout from Dick.

"Look!" cried the stout lad. "There's a fire! The grass is on fire, Bud!"

The western lad gave a quick look in the direction Dick indicated. It was off to the right from the trail they had been following.

"It is a fire - regular prairie fire," Bud murmured.

"Could any of the reservation Indians be on the rampage and have set it?" asked Nort.

"I don't know! We've got to find out about it!" shouted Bud. "Come on, fellows!" And, wheeling his horse, he abandoned the trail of the rustlers, and galloped toward the fire, followed by Nort and Dick.

Willard F. Baker

CHAPTER X

SERIOUS QUESTIONS

Some time before the boy ranchers reached the scene of the grass fire toward which they were riding, they caught the smell of the burning fodder. That it was only grass which was aflame they had known before this, for that was all there was to ignite in that section of the valley. There were no buildings as yet, tents taking their place. Though Bud and his father planned to erect substantial structures if this year was successful.

"A lot of good fodder going up in smoke, Bud!" yelled Nort, as he rode beside his cousin.

"If it isn't any worse than that we're lucky," was the answer.

"How do you mean?" asked Dick.

"I mean if we don't lose any cattle. The grass isn't any good after it dries up on the ground, the way this has. But if the fire starts a stampede of cattle - that will mean a loss."

"Do you think that's what the game is?" asked Nort, encouraging his pony, Blaze, by patting the animal's neck.

"I can't see what else it is, unless the fire started when some one threw down a burning match or cigarette, and most cow punchers aren't that careless. Our fellows wouldn't do it, and I don't believe any other ranchers around here would, except on purpose."

"You mean the Double Z bunch?" asked Dick.

"Sort of heading that way," replied Bud, significantly.

Together the boy ranchers rode on toward the fire, silently for a time, the only sounds being the thud of their ponies' feet and the creak of saddle leathers and stirrups. The smell of the burning grass was more pronounced now, and the pall of black smoke was rolling upward in a larger cloud.

"It's a big fire!" exclaimed Nort. "How can we stop it, Bud?"

"It will soon burn out," the western lad replied. "I happen to know where this grass is. It's a place where we couldn't very well bring water to, and if it doesn't rain much, as it hasn't lately, the fodder gets as dry as tinder. There's a sort of swale, or valley, filled with this dry grass and it's just naturally burning itself off."

"Then no very great harm will be done; will there?" asked Dick.

"Not much, unless the cattle get frightened and start to stampede. That's what I'm afraid of, and why I'm riding over there. We can't hope to put out the fire." Owing to the fact that the grass was so dry that no cattle would feed on it, there were no steers in the immediate vicinity of the blaze Had the fodder been cut it would have made excellent hay, but it would need to be cut green to bring this about. As it was, the tall grass had just naturally dried up as it attained its growth.

"It doesn't take even as much as a blaze like this to start a stampede," said Bud, as he and his cousins rode nearer to the burning grass, They could feel the heat of it, now. "It's queer how frightened animals are of fire," went on the rancher's son. "There must have been some wonderful sights out here, years ago, when there were millions of buffalo, and when there were prairie fires, miles in width, driving them before it."

"I should say so!" chimed in Nort. "I've read some of those stories in Cooper's books. He's great; isn't he!"

"You delivered the goods that time!" remarked Bud.

"I wish the west was like that now," voiced Dick. "With Indians and buffalo all over."

"There are a few Indians left yet," said Bud. "They're mostly on reservations, except when they make a break, ride off and act up bad. I guess we stock raisers are better off without the wild Indians.

"As for the buffalo, they were mighty valuable, and if we could raise them as well as cattle, we'd make a lot of money. The government is trying to get several herds started, but it's no easy task. Why, there are almost as many buffalo in New York city as there is out west now."

"Where!" asked Nort, not thinking for the moment.

"In Bronx Park," answered Bud. "I haven't seen 'em but I've read about 'em."

"Oh, yes. So have I," agreed Nort. "I forgot about them. Whew! It's getting hot," he added, as a shift in the wind brought into their faces a wave of heated and smoke-filled air.

"We'd better not keep on any nearer," decided Bud. "Let's ride around to the other side, and see what we can see."

Accordingly they turned to the right, as the fire seemed less fierce on that quarter, and continued on. They had been riding over a stretch of the valley carpeted with rich, dark green and fairly damp grass. Bud and his cousins knew that when the fire reached this stretch it would die out for lack of fuel.

In fact the blaze, as they could see, was confined to an area about a mile square, but of irregular shape. So far none of the cattle in sight had shown more than momentary fear of the blaze. They had run some distance from it and then stopped, sometimes going on with their eating, and again pausing to look with fear-widened eyes at the sight of the leaping tongues of fire.

"But we can't tell what's going on behind that smoke screen," declared Bud. "Some rustlers may have started it to hide their work."

"Any of your men over in that direction?" asked Dick.

"They aren't supposed to be," Bud replied. "Of course some of 'em may have ridden over when they saw the smoke, same as we did. But I don't see how any of 'em could have reached here as soon as we did."

Together they rode on, circling to the right to get around the edge of the fire.

"She's dying out," observed Dick.

"Yes, it can't burn much longer," admitted Bud. "And no great damage done, either, unless we find something we haven't yet seen."

But when they had completed the circuit around the edge of the blazing grass, and could ride across the fire-blackened area, and behind what was still a thick screen of smoke, they saw something which caused them great surprise.

This was not the sight of a bunch of stampeding cattle, though it was what Bud and his cousins folly; expected to encounter. There were some cattle on this side of the fire, but they had run far enough away to be out of danger, and beyond where they could be frightened into a frenzied rush.

"Look!" exclaimed Nort, pointing.

"Four Eyes!" exclaimed Dick.

"By the great horned toad and Zip Foster - yes!" agreed Bud, and his cousins knew he must be stirred to unusual depths of feeling to use this name. Zip Foster had not been mentioned in several weeks. The mysterious personage, on whom Bud called in times of great excitement, was almost a stranger, of late, in Happy Valley. In fact Dick and Nort never could get Bud to talk about Zip. But that is a story which will be told in its proper place, and due season.

"It *is* Four Eyes!" went on Bud, as he and his cousins recognized in the form of a distant rider that of Henry Mellon, the new cowboy. "And what he's doing here is more than I can imagine. I'm going to find out, though!"

The spectacled cow puncher was riding swiftly along, on a course that ran parallel to the direction of the fire. He was on the edge of the burned area, and galloping-away from the boys. But he was not beyond seeing or hailing distance.

"Hello there!" shouted Bud, dropping his reins and making a megaphone of his hands.

Four Eyes heard the call - there was no doubt of that, for he turned in his saddle and looked back. Then he must have seen the boys, for he waved his hat at them. Next he pointed ahead, as if to indicate that he was in pursuit of some one, and kept on, never slacking his pace.

"Come on!" shouted the impulsive Nort. "Let's catch up to him!"

He was about to spur his pony forward, but Bud caught the bridle.

"No use," said the western lad. "He's too far ahead, and our horses are too played out If he comes back well hear about it. If he doesn't -"

"Why, don't you think he'll come back!" interrupted Pick.

Willard F. Baker

"It wouldn't surprise me if he didn't," Bud answered. "There are some queer things going on around here, and he may be one of 'em. Though I haven't any reason to suspect him - yet!" he quickly added.

"What are we going to do!" asked Dick, as he saw his cousin slacking his pony's pace. "Shall we go on to the end of the rustler's trail, or follow Four Eyes."

"Neither one," answered Bud. "At least not just yet," he added, as he saw Nort and Dick look at him curiously. "Let Four Eyes go, for the time being. He may have seen some cowboys he'd like to interview about this fire, and be after them. Or he may not. As for getting on the trail of the rustlers, we'd have to ride back quite a distance to do that, and it would be dark when we picked it up again. Too late to do anything."

"Are we going back to camp?" asked Dick.

"No, let's stay right here. We've got grub, and water isn't so far off. We'll just camp out for the night."

"Suits me," assented Dick.

"Same here," agreed Nort.

It was something the boys had often done. They carried blankets and tarpaulins on their saddles, ready for this emergency, and they "packed" sufficient rations for several substantial, if not elaborate, meals. They had a coffee pot, a frying pan, bacon and prepared flour, and flapjacks were within their range of abilities as cooks.

Pausing to note that the fire was rapidly dying out, that

there was no cattle stampede in their vicinity, and noting that Four Eyes was now almost out of sight, the boy ranchers rode on to the nearest water-hole, and there prepared to spend the night, though it was still several hours until darkness should fall. But the horses were tired, for they had been run hard after the fire, and the boys decided to rest them. The lads, themselves, were fresh enough to have kept on, had there been occasion for it.

"Well, I'm glad this was no worse," observed Bud, as they sat down, having picketed their steeds, and looked at the receding pall of smoke. "I only hope the fellows at camp won't be worried."

"I guess they know we can take care of ourselves - at least we have so far," spoke Nort.

"Yes," agreed Bud. "You fellows have done pretty well since you came out here - you aren't tenderfeet any longer, not by all the shots that ever broke bottles."

"Say, what do you think of that, anyhow?" asked Dick, as he chewed reflectively on a bit of grass.

"I don't know what to think," asserted Bud. "There are a lot of serious questions we have to settle if we're going to keep on with this ranch."

"Why, we are going to keep on, aren't we?" asked Nort.

"I should say so!" cried Bud. "We're going to stick here, rustlers or not! And those are the only fellows I'm worrying about," and he tossed a lump of dirt in the fire which Dick was starting.

"Are there always rustlers to worry about on a ranch?" asked Nort.

"More or less," answered his cousin. "Especially when you have a place so near Double Z. I don't accuse Hank Fisher of being a rustler, exactly," he went on, "though I think Del Pinzo is. That's been proved, but it didn't do much good, for he broke jail and they can't seem to land him."

"What makes Hank Fisher and that Double Z bunch so sore at you?" asked Dick.

"I guess it's because we're beating them at the cattle game," answered Bud. "And because dad dammed the Pocut River and took some water for this valley. As if that hurt Hank!" he added. "But he makes that an excuse. However, I'll fight him to the finish!"

"And we're with you!" added Dick and Nort.

After supper they sat around the fire, talking of various matters. But ever and again the question troubled them of whether or not they could get on the trail of the rustlers. And, too, they wondered what could be the object of Four Eyes.

Night settled down, quiet save for the occasional snorting of the ponies. The boys wrapped themselves in their blankets and crawled between their tarpaulins with their feet to the smouldering fire. They talked until drowsiness stole over them and then, having decided to maintain no watch, they all three slumbered.

What time it was that Bud awakened he did not know. But awaken he did, and suddenly.

And the cause of his awakening was the sound of a horse rapidly ridden, and, evidently, approaching the place where he and his cousins had camped for the night.

"Who's there?" cried Bud suddenly, and without preface. Under the blanket his hand sought his weapon.

"Who's there!"

Willard F. Baker

CHAPTER XI

THE WATCH TOWER

Quickly the galloping hoofbeats came to a pause. With a motion of his foot, as he sat up amid his blanket and tarpaulin, Bud kicked into the fire a stick of greasewood which flared up, revealing a rider on a panting horse standing over the boy ranchers, all three of whom were now awake.

"Four Eyes!" cried Bud, for the flaring fire had revealed that cowboy. He had accepted his nickname in perfect grace.

"That's who," was the good-natured answer. "I saw the fire as I was riding back, and I thought you'd be here."

"Where were you riding *to*?" asked Bud, pointedly, his fingers releasing their grip on the .45 under the blanket. "I thought you were with Old Billee."

"I was supposed to be," answered Four Eyes, "until my horse got out of the corral and Billee said I could trail him. That's what I was doing when I saw you behind the fire. I knew it was almost burned out, so I didn't stop, or come back to explain."

"Yes, the fire didn't amount to much, though how it

was started is another question," said Bud. "You say your black horse got out?"

"Yes, jumped the corral fence. He's a bad one at that."

"You didn't get him back," observed Nort, for he and Dick, as well as Bud, had noticed that the new cow puncher bestrode one of the extra ponies kept at the camp corral for use in relieving the regular animals.

"No, he got clean away," and Henry Mellon did not seem to worry much about it. "All I have to say," he went on, "is that some one will get a mighty good mount, outside of his habit of jumping out of corrals."

"You may get him back - if whoever picks him up knows where he belongs," said Bud. For in that cow country it was still regarded as a great crime to steal a horse, or keep one known to belong to some one else.

"Oh, I'll prospect a bit farther for him tomorrow, maybe," said Four Eyes. "I didn't want to ride too far this evening, s I turned back. Did you get on any trail of the rustlers?" he asked, for he had been aware of the object of the boys' ride.

"We switched off to come over to the fire," said Bud. "Did you notice anything about it?"

"It was burning pretty good when I struck here, from over at your camp," was the answer. "I saw that it wasn't likely to do much damage, so I didn't ride back to tell Billee and the others."

"Did you see any one suspicious?" Bud went on, getting up and putting more wood on the fire.

"No, I didn't," answered Four Eyes, quietly. "Of course anyone would have had time to start the fire, and get well away before I arrived on the scene - judging by the way it was burning," he said. "Though I can't see what object anyone could have, and I'm inclined to think a passing cow puncher - not one of your crowd but some one else - may have flipped a cigarette butt into the grass where it smouldered for some time."

"That may have happened," Bud admitted. "As for an object, if the fire had stampeded the cattle it would have given some bunch of Greasers or rustlers a chance to get away with a few steers."

"Oh, yes, of course," agreed Four Eyes. "Well, I didn't see anybody. Guess I may as well turn in here. No use riding back to the camp to-night. It'll soon be morning."

"That's right, turn in," invited Bud. His suspicions had vanished.

"There's some cold coffee if you want it," added Nort.

"Guess I'll put it on to heat," said Henry Mellon. "It's a bit chilly."

"What time is it?" asked Dick, as the cowboy stirred up the embers and set the blackened coffee pot on over some stones that had been made into a rude fireplace.

"Two o'clock," announced Four Eyes, with a glance at his watch.

The boy ranchers watched him idly as he made and drank the coffee, munching some hard crackers he carried in one of his pockets. Then, rolling up in their blankets, the quartette went to sleep.

Morning came, in due course, without any untoward incidents having occurred. The boys looked across the fire-swept area to where, beyond it, many cattle could be observed grazing. There was no further vestige of fire. The heavy dew had extinguished the last, smouldering spark.

"Well, I'm going back to the camp," announced Four Byes, as they got the simple breakfast. And how appetizing was that aroma of sizzling bacon and strong coffee! "Want me to tell 'em anything for you!" he asked Bud.

"Tell 'em about the fire," was the request. "And say we're going on the trail of the rustlers. We'll be back to-day, though, around night, for we haven't grub enough to carry us farther."

"What you going to do about your horse?" asked Dick.

"What can I do?" asked Henry Mellon, in turn. "I can't spend all my time hunting him, when I've got to ride herd."

"We'll be on the lookout," Nort said.

"Hope you have luck," commented the strange cowboy, as he took off his glasses and wiped them on his silk neckerchief. "I'm lost without Cinder, though this pony isn't so bad," and he patted the neck of the animal he was riding.

A little later the boy ranchers were taking a short cut

across the fire-blackened strip, to get on the trail of the men who had driven off their cattle, while Four Eyes turned the head of his pony toward camp.

"Well, it looks as if this was where the trail ended," announced Bud, several hours later.

"Mighty funny, to come to an end so suddenly," commented Dick.

The three boys had reached one end of the many small valleys into which the larger vale was divided. They had been following the trail of the cattle that had been driven off - it was plain enough until they reached a rocky and shale-covered defile between two small hills. Then, for some reason or other, all "sign" came to an abrupt end. There were no further marks of hoofs in the earth, and none of the ordinary marks to indicate that cattle and horses had been beyond a certain point.

"It's just as Snake said," observed Dick. "They must have driven the animals here and then lifted them over the hill in an aeroplane."

"They couldn't!" declared Nort.

"I know they couldn't. But how else do you account for it?" asked his brother.

"They may have driven 'em through the pass, and then scattered dirt and stones over the trail to hide it," suggested Bud.

"Let's look a little farther then," remarked Dick.

They did, but without discovering any clues. It was as

though the rustlers had driven the cattle to the bottom of a rocky and bush-covered slope, and then as if the side of the hill had suddenly opened, providing a way through.

"Like some old fairy yarn!" declared Bud. "This gets me!"

"If we could only have gotten on the trail of the rascals sooner, Bud, we might have learned the secret," spoke Nort. "We ought to keep better watch!"

"How could we?" asked Bud. "We shoot off on the trail, now, as soon as we hear of anything."

"Yes, but we ought to get on the jump quicker," insisted his cousin. "If we had an airship, for instance!" and he laughed at the impracticability of his remark.

"You can see pretty nearly the whole of the valley from the top of Snake Mountain," spoke Dick, when he and Bud had joined in the laugh at Nort's airship idea. "If one of us could be up there -"

"We'd have to be there all the while!" interrupted Bud. "There's no telling when the rustlers will come. Talk about being on the watch! It's all right to say so, but how you going to work it?"

Dick suddenly uttered an exclamation.

"What's the matter?" his brother wanted to know. "See a snake?"

"No, but I've got the idea! A watch tower! Why not build one at our camp - or up on the side of the hill back of the reservoir? We could make it of logs - high enough to give us a good view. It wouldn't be much of a trick to climb up in the watch tower three or four times a day and survey the place. A watch tower is the thing, Bud!"

CHAPTER XII

IN SPITE OF ALL

Nort and Bud stared at Dick for several seconds without making any remark. They were sitting on their ponies, completely baffled by the manner in which the trail of the rustlers had suddenly "petered out." And they had been about to turn and go back to camp when Dick made his enthusiastic remark.

"A watch tower?" repeated Bud.

"Sure!" declared his cousin. "We used to build 'em when I belonged to the Boy Scouts. Remember, Nort?"

"Sure! It begins to come back to me. We used to bind saplings together and make quite a high perch. The idea was that you might be able to see your way if you got lost," he explained to Bud.

"Not a bad idea, either," commented the western lad. "I begin to see your drift, as the wind said to the snowstorm. You mean to build a sort of high platform up by the reservoir, Dick?"

"Yes, a watch tower of logs, strong enough to hold one or two fellows. You could make ladders so's we could reach the top platform, or we could scramble up if we

Willard F. Baker

left hand and foot holds where we lopped the branches off saplings." "That's right!" cried Bud, now almost as enthusiastic as was his cousin. "And with a good pair of glasses, or a telescope such as dad has at the ranch, we could see all over the valley."

"Let's make it!" cried Nort, and the matter was settled as quickly as that.

Something of the excitement that had moved them must have been visible on the faces of the boys when they returned to camp, for Old Billee, greeting them in the absence of the other cowboys, asked:

"Did you land 'em, Bud?"

"Who; the rustlers? No. Couldn't see where they'd vanished to any more than, as one of the boys said, as if an airship had been used. But we got an idea, Billee."

"They're valuable - sometimes," agreed the veteran cow puncher cautiously.

"We hope this one is going to be!" frankly laughed Bud. "We're going to build a watch tower, and take turns staying up in it with a telescope. We can see almost the whole valley if we get high enough, and as there aren't many patches of woodland where the rascals can hide, we hope to spot the rustlers as soon as they begin their tricks."

"Well, you may do it," and again the cowboy was very cautious. "I never heard of cattle rustlers bein' caught that way, but when other means fail, try suthin' diffrunt! We'll tackle th' tower!"

And as the other cowboys, even Four Eyes, pronounced the scheme worth trying, it was put into operation. Mr. Merkel, to whom Bud communicated his idea over the telephone, rather laughed at it.

"How about nights?" asked the ranchman. "No matter how high you are up after dark you can't see any better."

"But most of the raids of the rustlers have been in daylight," declared Bud.

"It's about fifty-fifty," his father told him. "However, it won't do any harm to try it. Only don't fall off that watch tower of yours. I'll come out and look at it when you get it done."

The boy ranchers and their cow punchers started work the next day. Dick and Nort remembered, in a dim way, how, as Boy Scouts, they had helped erect towers, hastily constructed of saplings. Their recalled knowledge, together with the natural adaptability and skill of the cowboys, finally succeeded in there being evolved, and erected, on the aide of the valley rather a pretentious tower. "It must look like an oil well derrick from a distance," observed Nort, when it was al most completed.

"What do we care how it looks, if it does the trick?" retorted Bud. "From that perch, and with this telescope dad let me take, I can tell the color of a cow clear to the end of our valley."

There was no question but what the watch tower did provide an excellent vantage point. From its top platform, reached by rude ladders, any unusual movement in the entire valley could be seen during the day.

It was planned that the boys - and by this I mean the hired cowboys also - should take turns in being on watch in the tower during certain periods each day. A schedule was drawn up by Bud and his cousins, and put into operation as soon as the tower was completed.

"And now we'll catch the rustlers at work!" boasted Bud.

But alas for their hopes! In spite of all their precautions, and setting at naught the hard work of constructing the tower, there was another raid on the cattle in Happy Valley, about a week after the wooden perch had been set up.

It was not a disastrous raid, and only a half score of steers were driven off from one of the more distant herds. But the raid took place, and at night. It was discovered one morning, just as Bud was going up into the tower, where a scat and sheltered place had been built.

"They fooled us, Bud," said Old Billee, riding in from a distant part of the valley.

"Fooled us? How?"

"They let us watch by day, an' they come an' robbed by night! Another bunch of steers gone!"

"Well - by Zip Foster!" cried Bud, slamming his hat down on the ground. "I'm getting tired of this!"

CHAPTER XIII

THE SIGNAL

"What's the matter?" cried Dick, hastening from the tent where he had been making a new loop on his lariat, in preparation for practicing some of the stunts worked by Four Eyes.

"Have you discovered something from the tower?" asked Nort.

"Yes, I've discovered that the tower isn't any good!" exclaimed Bud with emphasis. "Oh, it isn't your fault, Dick," he went on, as he saw that his cousin looked a bit crestfallen. "The tower is all right."

"Then you saw some rustlers from it?" asked Nort.

"No, that's the trouble," said Bud, ruefully. "We didn't see them but they were here all right - last night. Tell us about it, Billee," he requested.

"Well, there isn't an awful lot to tell," said the veteran cow puncher. "I was just prospectin' around, over on that new growth of Johnson grass, like you told me to, an' I saw where a steer had been killed, an' they had eat most of it, too, by th' signs."

Willard F. Baker

"You mean the rustlers?" asked Nort.

"Rustlers, Greasers, Del Pinzo's bunch - anything you like t' call 'em," asserted Billee. "Somebody, that hadn't any right t' do it, druv off our cattle!"

"And I say it's about time it was stopped!" declared Bud with as great positiveness as before. This time he picked up the hat he had dashed to the ground and dusted it off. "I'm going to do something desperate!" he declared.

"What, son?" asked Old Billee mildly. "They's allers been rustlers in this cow country, an' they'll allers be some, I reckon. Course if you can git 'em in th' _act_, they's nothin' t' do but shoot 'em up. But when you can't git 'em -"

"That's what I'm going to do!" declared Bud. "I'm going to get on the trail of these rustlers and clean 'em out! Tell us more about it, Billee. No use getting up in the watch tower now," he added, gloomily enough. "We've got other work cut out for us. Go ahead, Billee! Shoot!"

"Let me give you a word of advice first, Buddy boy," spoke the veteran cowboy as he slowly got off his pony, an act of grace for which the animal was, doubtless, duly thankful. Billee was no featherweight, though he was as active as need be, in spite of his bulk.

"What's the advice?" asked Bud good-naturedly. His first hot anger was beginning to cool.

"Well, my advice is to leave these rustler alone," said Old Billee. "They's allers been rustlers here an' they'll allers be here. Every cow country has 'em. They're like th' old pirates that used t' hold up th' ships. Taking tribute, so t' speak."

"But our country didn't pay that tribute long!" exclaimed Dick, remembering the brilliant exploits of Decatur against the corsains of Algiers, Tunis and Tripoli. "'Millions for defense, but not a cent for tribute'!" quoted Dick in a ringing voice.

"That's what I say!" chimed in Nort.

"Well, it *is* tribute, in a way," admitted Old Billee. "I was going t' say if you'd let th' rustlers make off with a few steers now an' then it would save trouble. They're used t' takin' a few. But if you fight 'em then they'll make a big raid with a big gang, an' mebby, take all you got, Bud!"

"I'd like to see 'em try it!" cried the western lad. "And I won't sit by and have my cattle stolen; will we, fellows?" he appealed to his cousins.

"Not on your life!" declared Nort and Dick.

"Well, I shore do like t' hear you talk that-a-way," said Old Billee. "I didn't think you'd do it. Course it ain't no fun t' sit still an' let these onery Greasers walk off with your cattle. But, as I say, it's sometimes easier'n 'tis t' fight 'em. Lots of th' ranchmen do pay tribute in a way. Your father was one of th' fust t' fight 'em, Bud, but even he has sorter give up now, an' he don't raise no terrible row when a few of his steers get hazed off."

"Well, dad has more, and losing a few doesn't put a crimp in him," said Bud. "It's different with us, and I'm

Willard F. Baker

not going to stand it. Zip Foster wouldn't and I'm not going to!" and again he dashed his hat on the ground, thereby startling Billee's horse.

"Say, why don't you get Zip Foster over to help chase the rustlers?" asked Dick, slyly nudging Nort. They had long been trying to get Bud to a "show down" on the identity of this mysterious personage.

"Oh, I reckon we can do it ourselves," and Bud seemed to regret mentioning the name of his favorite.

"Just what are you aimin' t' do, son?" asked Billee, as Snake and Yellin' Kid rode up, ready for their day's work out on the range among the cattle.

"I don't exactly know, but it's going to be something and something hard!" asserted Bud. "Are there any clues over there, Billee, to give us a lead?"

"Not many, Bud. Just th' usual. They come onto a few scattered steers, killed one roasted what they wanted of it, slipped off the hide an' left th' rest t' th' buzzards. Then they druv off th' remainder. I didn't foller th' trail, for I could see they was half a dozen rustlers in th' bunch, an' it ain't exactly healthy for one man t' trail a crowd like that even if he was a two-gun man, which I don't lay no claim t' bein' no how," concluded the veteran modestly. They all knew he would be brave enough in an even fight. But they all recognized the fact that it would have been foolish for him, alone, to have attempted to trail a gang of desperate men.

"Well, I'm going to see what we can do," Bud declared. "If you've sized up all there was to see over there, Billee," and he nodded in the direction of the latest raid on Diamond X Second, "there's no use in me going over. I think I'll go have a talk with dad," he concluded. "I want action!"

"So do we!" added Dick.

"Then come along!" invited his cousin.

A little later the boy ranchers were riding out of the valley, on their way to the main ranch of Diamond X. They would not be back until late that night, or, possibly, until the following morning, for Bud wanted to have a good, long talk with his father, and decide on some plan of action, that would drive out the rustlers and keep them away.

As Old Billee had said, probably an older and more experienced rancher would have put up with a few losses for the sake of peace and quietness. But Bud, like most lads of his age, was impulsive. And, as he had said, the loss of even a few steers meant possible failure to him and his cousins, just starting in the ranch business as they were.

"Was that a black one?" suddenly asked Bud, as Nort's horse shied at something.

"A black what!" Nort wanted to know.

"A black jack rabbit that ran across the trail in front of you just now," Bud resumed. "If it was, it will bring bad luck, as Old Billee would say," and he laughed.

"No, it was a sort of gray one, part white," Nort answered, for it was one of those immense hares that had leaped across the trail, almost under the feet of

Willard F. Baker

his pony.

"That means we'll have part bad luck and part good," declared Dick.

And some hours later, when they had reached Bud's home, and Nell was serving peach pie and glasses of milk to the boy ranchers, Nort paused long enough in his eating to remark:

"*This* is the good luck, Bud."

"You declaimed something that time!" agreed his brother.

Mr. Merkel listened to what Bud and his cousins told them of the raids on Happy Valley.

"Well, you haven't suffered any more than the average ranchman, just starting in," said Bud's father. "The rustlers always seem to pick on a newcomer."

"Well, they'll find I'm a sort of prickly pear to pick on!" asserted Bud. "Dad, can't we clean out these rascals?"

"Well, it's your ranch, Bud! You can do anything you like, within reason, but I wouldn't like to see you take any foolish risks."

"There's got to be some risks," declared Bud. "I'm not looking to get out of 'em. But don't you think it would be a good thing if we could get rid of this Del Pinzo gang for good?"

"Sure, Bud. I'll give you all the help I can, and I'll

spare you one or two more men if you need 'em - for a time, that is, as we're pretty busy here."

"All right. When we're ready I'll call on you," said Bud, as though he had great plans in preparation. As a matter of fact, as he admitted later, he really did not know what he was going to do, but he was not going to admit that to his father. In other words he was "putting up a bluff," and I have some reason for suspecting that Mr. Merkel knew this. However he gave no sign. In spite of the pie, cake and other good things set out by Nell and Mrs. Merkel, Bud and his chums decided to ride back to their camp that night. It was dark at the start, but the moon would be up later, and the trail was well known.

The boy ranchers rode leisurely along, for there was no special hurry in getting back. It might reasonably be supposed that the rustlers would not again make a raid within a few days at least. And Old Billee, Yellin' Kid, Snake Purdee and Four Eyes, to say nothing of Buck Tooth, were well able to look after matters in Happy Valley.

And thus proceeding at a foot pace, it was well after midnight when the boys started down the last slope that led into the valley proper. In daylight it would have been possible, from this part of the trail, to have observed the tents and the reservoir. But now all was shrouded in darkness.

No, not altogether darkness, for as the boys rode forward there suddenly glimmered in the gloom a light, high up in the air. At first Bud thought it was a star, but a moment later as it moved from side to side, and then up and down, he exclaimed:

"Look, fellows! A signal!"

"Signal!" repeated Dick.

"Yes. Over at our camp! See! There's a light on our watch tower."

"Maybe there's been another raid!" said Nort.

"Or going to be one!" spoke Bud, grimly.

CHAPTER XIV

FOUR EYES - NO EYES

Thudding along, their ponies seemingly as eager to reach the ranch camp as were the boys themselves, Bud, Nort and Dick raced toward the mysterious light. For that it was mysterious they all agreed, and that it was flashing from the top of the watch tower they had built to spy for rustlers was another conclusion.

"Do you s'pose it can be Old Billee, or Yellin' Kid signalling to us?" asked Nort, as he galloped between Bud and Dick.

"They wouldn't know we were coming," Bud answered. "I said we might not be back until tomorrow."

"That's so. But who do you think is signalling?" asked Dick.

"And who are they signalling to?" Nort wanted to know. "That's what we've got to find out," spoke Bud, grimly. "And it's what we're going to find out in a short time! Come on, Sock!" he called to his pony. "This is only exercise for you!"

Indeed the animals had not been hard pressed, and this

Willard F. Baker

burst of speed was rather a relief than anything else. Together the boy ranchers hastened toward their camp.

For some time the lantern - it was evidently that and not a torch - was waved to and fro, parallel to the horizon, and again up and down. It was so evidently a signal, or a series of them, that the boys no longer questioned this theory.

But who the signaller was, and to whom he was flashing his message in the dark night - those were other questions. And they were questions that needed answering.

"It must be one of our men," remarked Bud. "No one else could get into camp and climb the tower without a row being raised."

"How do you know there hasn't been a row?" asked Dick.

"What do you mean?" countered Bud.

"I mean there may have been a fight," Dick went on. "Maybe the rustlers have surprised our camp, put Yellin' Kid and the rest of our bunch out of business and are signalling to the main crowd to come up and drive off the cattle. I might as well say that as think it," he added. "And that's what I've been thinking the last few minutes."

This dire suggestion struck Bud and Nort silent for a moment. And then, more because he did not want to believe it, than because he did not believe it possible, Bud exclaimed: "I don't believe any such thing!"

"I don't want to believe it!" said Nort. "But of course there may have been a fight."

"If there was, there's a lot of dead Greasers and rustlers scattered around, you can depend on that!" declared Bud, grimly.

"Yes, I reckon Old Billee, Snake and the rest would give a good account of themselves," asserted Dick.

"And they wouldn't be taken by surprise, either," added Nort.

"Not likely," affirmed his cousin.

Again they directed their gaze toward the flashing signal on the tower. Once more they saw it slowly raised and lowered, and then swept from side to side.

"Are they spelling out a message in Morse or Continental code?" asked Bud.

"It does look like the Morse," said Nort. "We learned that when we were Boy Scouts. I can make out some letters, but they don't spell anything that has any sense to it."

"Maybe it's in Spanish," suggested Bud, who was not familiar with the method of spelling words by flags or lanterns. "There's a lot of Greasers around here who don't know anything but Spanish."

"That's so," agreed Nort. "I didn't think of that. I'll try and catch what the next word is, and maybe you'll know it, Bud," for the western lad understood some of the language of Mexico.

But just when Nort was directing his attention to the signal flashes Dick, who had ridden on a little ahead, suddenly called:

"Is that a fire?"

They looked to where he pointed and, for a moment, thought it was another blaze in the dried grass. For the eastern skyline that had been only dimly seen was now outlined in a red flare.

"It is a fire!" asserted Nort.

"It's the moon rising!" said Bud.

And so it proved. The moon was coming up, big, round and red, and, when below the horizon, cast a reflection not unlike a fire. The boys laughed with relieved spirits as they rode on. But when Nort next directed his attention to the flashing lantern it was no longer signalling. In the direction of the watch tower there was only blackness, for the moon's rays had not yet reached it.

"Looks as if they'd quit," said Dick.

"Maybe they thought the moonlight would give 'em away," suggested Nort.

"We'll soon know about it," declared Bud, with grim meaning.

They were now within a short distance of the tents, gleaming white in the moonbeams. From one of the larger canvas shelters shone a ruddy light, showing dark figures within. And then was borne to the ears of the boys the sound of laughter.

"That doesn't seem to indicate a raid or fight," spoke Nort.

"You can't be sure," Bud remarked. "We'd better be careful. Let's dismount and go on foot."

They left their ponies, throwing the reins over the heads of the animals, and cautiously approached the tents of the cow punchers on foot. This tent was, practically, the "bunk house," the assembling place of the men after their hours of work. But before the boys reached this their approach was evidently heard. For a figure came to the flap and a challenging voice called:

"Who's there?"

"Old Billee!" cried Bud, as he and his chums recognized the tones, and with the recognition came a sense of relief.

"Oh, you're back; are you, Bud?" asked the veteran cowboy. "I thought I heard some one."

"Who's up on the watch tower with a lantern?" called Bud, once it was certain that no disaster had occurred.

"Watch tower?" repeated Yellin' Kid, coming to the flap to stand beside Old Billee.

"Lantern?" added Snake.

"Somebody's signalling," went on Bud.

"You'd better come out and we'll have a look. Are you

all here?"

"All of us," answered Old Billee. "Come on, Four Eyes!" he cried. "Tumble out of your bunk. There's somethin' doin'!"

"Four Eyes must have gone to bed early," said Bud to his cousins as they stood outside the tent. For Billee's call indicated that the spectacled cowboy had retired.

"Hi! Four Eyes!" shouted Yellin' Kid, in a voice that would have awakened the proverbial Seven Sleepers. "Turn out!"

There was a moment's pause, during which Buck Tooth came up to the bunk tent from his own special nook for sleeping. And then, the voice of Snake Purdee announced:

"Four Eyes isn't here!"

"Isn't here!" repeated Billee. "Why, I saw him turn in a while ago, when we started t' play cards."

"He isn't here now," declared Snake. "His bunk is empty, and he didn't go out the front way, I'll wager on that. There's something queer going on all right!"

CHAPTER XV

A BIG RAID

Into the bunk tent of the older cowboys crowded the young ranch lads. Doubt, suspicion and wonder mingled in their minds, and foremost of all were two outstanding matters - the mysterious signalling light, and the disappearance of Four Eyes - if, indeed, that individual had really taken himself off.

"Are you sure he was here?" asked Bud, when, after the first break of surprise, questions were in order.

"Sure," replied Yellin' Kid. "We all come in here, after th' chores was done, t' have a friendly game of cards an' smoke. We didn't look for you back until late, if at all."

"And was Four Eyes with you then?" asked Nort.

"You couldn't exactly say he was _with_ us," replied Snake. "An' yet he wasn't *away* from us. He pretended he didn't want t' play cards, an' he said he was so doggoned tired an' sleepy that he was goin' t' turn in. I told him that bein' in th' same tent with a whisperin' infant like Yellin' Kid, wasn't perzactly healthy for sleep, but Four Eyes said he didn't mind. So he turned int' his bunk, an' pulled th' covers tip over his head,

Willard F. Baker

though I don't see how he stood it, for it isn't winter, not by a long shot, an' this place was full of smoke. Anyhow he done it, an' t' keep th' light out of his eyes, so he said, he pulled a chair up in front of his bunk like you see it now, an' stuck his coat over it."

Snake pointed to a chair, now twisted awry from in front of the cot that the missing cowboy had occupied. His coat, draped over the back, effectually screened him from observation when lying on the bed.

"He did that so's he could slip out an' get away!" spoke Yellin' Kid, justifying the sarcastic name of "whispering infant," that Snake had bestowed on him.

"But how did he get out?" asked Dick.

"And what for?" Bud wanted to know,

"He got out this way!" said Old Billee quietly, as he leaned over the cot and pushed with his hand against the side of the tent. A right-angled opening was disclosed, cut with a sharp knife. The loose point was at the bottom, and once Four Eyes had slipped out, the cut flap hung down in place, not disclosing, in the dim light, that the canvas had been cut.

"He got out that way," went on Old Billee, "because th' tent sides, bein' fast t' th' board floor, wouldn't let him crawl out very easy. He's a slick one, Four Eyes is!"

"But why should he slip out this way? Did he do anything? And who was doing that signalling?" exclaimed Bud.

"I reckon you'll find, son, that the signallin' an' th'

vamoosin' of our late friend Four Eyes had some connection," spoke Old Billee. "We, bein' intent on our game of cards, didn't know nothin' at all 'bout it till you fellows rode up. Now it's about time we got int' action!"

"You win!" declared Yellin' Kid loudly. "There's suthin' queer prospectin' around these diggings an' I'd like t' know what it is!"

"I guess we all would," spoke Bud. "And we'd better start right in to find out about it. Come on, boys," he called to his cousins, but the older cow punchers took the invitation to themselves also, and soon, with lanterns and flashlights (which handy little contrivances the boy ranchers nearly always carried) they began the search.

First they made sure that Four Eyes was playing no trick on them by hiding under one of the cots in the bunk tent. Though, as Bud pointed out, it would pass the bounds of fun to have cut the canvas shelter as it was cut.

But no trace of Four Eyes was to be found.

"He's gone, hide, hair, horns, brand an' everythin'!" was the way Old Billee expressed it.

"How about his horse?" asked Nort.

"He didn't get his black one back," remarked Snake. "But he may have sort of helped himself to one of yours, Bud."

This was found to be the case when the corral was

visited. It could hardly have been expected, in that country of great distances, that the missing cowboy would not take a horse.

"And now let's have a look at the tower," suggested Bud, when a rapid survey, under the fitful moonlight, had been made in the vicinity of the camp, and no trace of the missing man discovered. "Some one was signalling from up there, and it must have been Four Eyes."

"It *could* have been some one else," suggested Dick, not because he believed that, but because he wanted to sift all the evidence and get to the bottom of matters.

"Yes, it may have been a wandering cowboy, Greaser or some Indian, far from his native reservation," Bud admitted. "But I'm saying it was Four Eyes, though why he did it I can't imagine."

Nor could any of the others. Or, if they had a theory, they did not give voice to it, though, afterward, one and all said they had associated the missing cowboy with the rustlers.

But a search on and near the hastily-built watch tower disclosed nothing. On the top platform, whence, doubtless, the signalling lantern had been waved, no light was found. There were burned matches and cigarette stubs, to be sure, but these were as much the discarded property of Yellin' Kid or Snake, as of Four Eyes, for they all had taken turns doing sentry duty, and, as it was lonesome up on the high perch, smoking was indulged in.

"Well, he's away, and that's all there is to it," said Bud,

when the search was over. "Now all we've got to do is to wait for something to happen."

"Do you think something will happen?" asked Nort.

"Well, things have been happening ever since we came out here," observed Dick. "First it was the finding of the Triceratops. Then it was the water fight in the mysterious tunnel, and now it's the rustlers after our cattle. Isn't that enough to happen?"

"Oh, yes," admitted Nort. "But I thought Bud meant something special was about due."

"It wouldn't surprise me if it did happen," declared the western lad. "But I wasn't thinking of anything out of the usual. Only the combination - Four Eyes missing and us seeing the light makes me suspicious. So I'm ready for anything."

"And I'm ready for my bunk!" declared Dick, with a yawn. "It's most morning! Let's turn in!"

They did, but none of the boy ranchers rested well, for they were too worried.

What did it all mean? And what events portended? These were questions they wished soon would be answered.

The morning did not bring the return of Four Eyes, nor in the better light were any more clues discovered at the Watch Tower. Looking from its height, over the peaceful valley, the boy ranchers saw nothing evil, and there was no hint of coming disaster other than in the suspicions engendered by the recent strange happenings.

"Do you suppose that signalling could have meant an Indian uprising?" asked Nort.

"Cracky! If it does we'll have to fight 'em, won't we?" asked Dick, with sparkling eyes.

"I don't imagine the Indians around here have any notion of rising," said Bud. "They have done such things, years ago, but I doubt if they have enough spirit left for it now. They are too well satisfied with their lot. But of course it's possible, though Buck Tooth says he doesn't look for anything of the sort. But then he's been with white men so long he isn't really much of an Indian any more."

"Well, if there's any Indian fighting to be done I want to do my share!" declared Dick, and his brother nodded in confirmation.

But as several days passed, and nothing more happened than the usual hard work on the ranch, the apprehensions of the boys began to disappear. They made inquiries about Four Eyes, but no one on the neighboring ranches had seen him. Mr. Merkel expressed himself as greatly disappointed in the character of the cowboy he had sent to his son.

"Maybe you got off lucky, with only a cut tent," the ranchman observed. "But better be on your guard, son."

"We will, Dad," replied the western lad.

It was about a week after the signal lights had been

observed, the disappearance of Four Eyes coinciding, that, as Bud and his cousins were eating "grub" in camp one noon, they heard shots fired off to the north, and in the direction of the trail between Happy Valley and Diamond X ranch.

"What's that?" asked Nort, starting from his seat.

"Stampede, maybe," suggested Dick, for the boys knew that the older cowboys were in that direction, rounding up a small herd which had been purchased and that was to be shipped east. Bud hurried to the entrance of the tent and what he saw caused him to cry:

"Come on, boys! It's the rustlers again! They're making a raid! Get your guns!"

In less time than you would have deemed possible, unless you had seen it, the boy ranchers were in the saddle, and were galloping toward the scene of the shooting. The sounds were more plain, now, and as they straightened out on the trail they could see where a fight was in progress.

Willard F. Baker

CHAPTER XVI

ON THE TRAIL

Yellin' kid, Old Billee and Snake Purdee were standing off the attacks of more than double their number. This was the spectacle that greeted Bud, Nort and Dick as they swept up the trail and toward the sound and sight of the firing. For now they could see the little puffs of smoke which preceded the discharges of the guns. Light, traveling faster than sound, brought to the eyes of the boys the puffs of burned gunpowder before the report echoed.

"This is the meaning of that night-signalling!" cried Nort, as he galloped beside his cousin.

"Looks so," was the answer. "They're getting bold and desperate to try to rustle our stock in the day time."

"You said it!" exclaimed Dick, as he looked to make sure he had a good supply of cartridges.

As the boy ranchers drew nearer the scene of the conflict they could observe that the herd, which their cowboys had been driving in, was now in confusion. And no wonder, with more than half a score of wildly-excited men riding among them, shouting and firing heavy revolvers.

For distant shouts borne to the ears of our heroes told of the excitement under way. As nearly as Bud, Nort and Dick could tell from their vantage point, eight or ten Mexicans, Greasers or other undesirable characters, had swept down from the north on Old Billee, Snake and Yellin' Kid as the latter were hazing the cattle along to the trail which led to the distant railroad station. Naturally the cowboys of Happy Valley had turned on their attackers and the fight resulted.

It was evidently the intention of the rustlers (for of their character there was little doubt) to drive off as many of the Diamond X Second stock as possible. And if they had to kill or maim the watchers it meant little to them.

But, so far, none seemed to have been seriously hurt, for no horses were running around with empty saddles, and no bodies were prostrate on the ground. I think, if the truth were known, that the first shooting on both sides was so wild that no one thought to take accurate aim, which is difficult on the back of a rushing cow pony, and with a heavy .45 gun.

It was, essentially, a running fight and Bud, Dick and Nort were urging their ponies forward as rapidly as possible to get their share of it. However, they were not destined to come to close grips with the enemy. For as they drew nearer to the scene of conflict, their guns out, and eager in their own hearts for action, yelling encouragement to their comrades, the boy ranchers saw their foes suddenly swing away.

This sudden giving up on the part of the rustlers was due either to a signal from one of their number that the raid was a failure, or else they saw reinforcements, in the persons of the boys, and had no desire for a more nearly even battle.

At any rate, with wild yells, the rustlers pulled up their ponies, and turned off down the trail, riding at breakneck speed. Yellin' Kid and Snake, with shouts of defiance, swept after them, and might have caught them except for what happened to Old Billee. The veteran suddenly reeled in his saddle, and would have fallen, except that, as he lagged behind his two companions, Bud rushed up to him and held him in place.

"Are you hit, Billee?" Bud cried.

"Only just a scratch, but it seems like it took th' tucker out o' me mighty suddin," gasped the old man. "Beckon I'd better get down. I'd 'a' fallen if you hadn't rid up, Bud."

"That's what I thought when I saw you reel."

By the time Bud, with his cousins, was helping Old Billee to the ground, Yellin' Kid and Snake turned and saw what had happened. They then gave up all thoughts of pursuing the retreating rustlers and came riding back, winded and excited, but none the worse for their encounter with the rascals.

"Did they get you, Billee?" asked Snake, a gleam in his eyes that portended no good to the perpetrators of the deed if he ever caught them.

"Only a scratch," said the old cowboy, but rather faintly. He put his hand to his side, and quickly opening his garments, as he sat on the ground, his friends saw that the wound was more than that.

However, the bullet had glanced off the ribs, and aside from having lost considerable blood, which accounted for his weakness, Old Billee was little the worse off.

"I think we got one of 'em," announced Snake. "I saw him holdin' pretty desprit like t' his saddle."

"What started it? Who were they?" asked Bud, as the last of the raiders swept out of sight amid the rolling hills of the valley.

"Oh, some of Del Pinzo's gang, you can make sure of that," said Yellin' Kid. "They just rid down on us an' started t' fire. We saw what their game was all right, an' come back at 'em. They didn't get one steer, Bud!" he added, proudly enough.

"That's good," said the boy rancher.

"But they did an awful lot of shootin'," added Snake. "I thought sure we'd all be hit, but Old Billee was th' only one what got it. I never heard so much Fourth of July since I was a kid."

"It was a lot of shooting, according to the results," spoke Bud, as he watched Snake bandaging Billee's wound, for the cowboys carried a primitive first-aid kit. "I wonder if that meant anything?"

"What do you mean?" asked Nort.

But Bud did not answer.

Making sure that none of the cattle had been hit, and

Willard F. Baker

managing, after rather strenuous work, in quieting the herd, the boy ranchers and their friends started back toward camp, Old Billee taking it as easily as possible, for his side was getting stiff and painful.

While they were yet some distance away from the white tents that corresponded to the usual ranch buildings, Bud and his companions saw riding toward them a solitary figure.

"It's Buck Tooth," declared Dick.

"And if he doesn't bear evil tidings I miss my guess," murmured Bud.

Evil tidings they were, in very truth. For as the Zuni came near enough he was seen to be much excited. Drawing rein, he made a sweeping, comprehensive gesture with one hand, toward the south end of the valley, and exclaimed: "All gone!"

"What's all gone?" asked Bud, a great fear clutching at his heart.

"Cattle!" answered the Indian. "Rustlers drive 'em all 'way, while you shootin' off there!" and he pointed toward the scene of the recent conflict.

For an instant Bud said nothing. Then, with trembling lips, which alone betrayed his feeling, he remarked:

"That was it! They divided their gang and started a fake fight up at one end, to draw us there, while they worked against our big herd at the other end. It was a slick piece of work. No wonder they shot more than they hit. They wanted to keep us away from the south of the valley."

"I guess you've struck it, Bud," said Snake, grimly. "They sure fooled us, an' I never smelled a rat! Whew!"

Bud, with lips that were firmer now, touched spurs to his pony and hastened toward the tents and corral.

"What you aimin' to do?" called Yellin' Kid after him.

"I'm going to get on the trail of those rustlers," grimly announced Bud Merkel, "and I'm not coming back until I land 'em! Come on, fellows," he called to his cousins. "Let's pack up for a long hike on the trail!"

Willard F. Baker

CHAPTER XVII

WILD COUNTRY

Following after Bud, his cousins and the older cowboys swept along toward the home camp - to the tents which served the purposes of ranch buildings. Yellin' Kid trotted beside Old Billee, who, however, now that his bullet-scarred side had been bandaged, rode with more ease.

"What you goin' t' stop for?" asked Snake, when he saw Bud turning in toward the corral where spare ponies were kept. "Aren't you going after the rustlers?"

"Yes, when we get packed up for a long ride!" Bud answered grimly. "What's the good of riding over just to look at the place where they drove off our cattle? I can see that any time. What I want to do is to get on their trail."

"And not give up until we land 'em!" added Nort.

"That's talking!" cried his brother. "Did you see any of 'em, Buck Tooth?" he asked the Indian, beside whom he was riding.

"Me see too many," was the grim answer, which explained why the Zuni had probably not gone in pursuit. "They ride like what you call - jack-rabbits."

"They can't keep that pace up long," declared Bud, as he slipped from the saddle, having turned his horse into the corral. "They can start the steers off with a hip-hurrah, but they'll have to slow down if they don't want to kill 'em, and that wouldn't pay. They'd get some fresh beef and the hides, but they'd waste more than they'd get out of it."

"What do you imagine they really plan to do, and who are they?" asked Dick, as he and his brother followed Bud to their own special tent.

"I can only guess who they are, and your guess is as good as mine," the western lad answered.

"Then I'll say Del Pinzo and the Hank Fisher gang," ventured Nort.

"And I'll agree," replied Bud. "They have two motives, now, for working against us. One because we've beaten 'em in two innings - the time of the Triceratops and in the underground river game. But getting our cattle - or the cattle of any other rancher - is reward enough in itself at the price beef is selling for now. They want to make a lot of money, and ruin us because we've come to Happy Valley. But they'll find that we can bat a little, too," added Bud, carrying out the simile of a baseball game. "And it's going to be our turn at the plate mighty soon!"

"The sooner the better," declared Nort, and his brother nodded in agreement.

When Old Billee's wound had been further attended to,

with the more adequate remedies kept in camp, there was a gathering of the "clan," so to speak, in the tent where the boys and their cowboy helpers usually ate.

"Then you aren't going to chase over to where they drove off your cattle right away; is that it, Bud?" asked Snake.

"I don't see any use," said the young western ranch lad. "All we'd see would be the marks of the trail, and they'll stay for some time, if it doesn't rain, which isn't likely. What I want to do is to pack enough grub - and other things," he added significantly with a motion toward his .45, "for a long trip. We've got to get at the bottom of how they drive off our cattle, and manage to get them out of the valley without leaving a trace.

"That's the puzzle we have to solve, as we found out about the hidden water. Up to now the raids of Del Pinzo and his crowd - assuming that they are the ones - have been small. They're the kind that's always going on, and a lot of the cattlemen, and Dad among 'em, seem to shut their eyes to the thefts. I'm not going to do that. But what I started to say was that, up to now, the raids have been small ones. Very likely they thought we wouldn't make much fuss over the steers we lost.

"But this is a big raid, and the others were only leading up to it. They played to get us out of the south end of the valley, and away from our big herd so they could drive it off unmolested."

"And they sure did it," added Nort.

"But they haven't gotten clear away yet!" snapped out

Bud. "We're going to take after them! They can't go fast with a big bunch of cattle, and we're bound to catch them sooner or later!"

"They'll probably put up a fight," observed Old Billee, who was feeling much easier, now.

"That's what I'm counting on, and that's why I don't want any slip-up!" exclaimed Bud. "I'm going to call on Dad for some reinforcements."

"Oh, we can handle that Del Pinzo gang!" boasted Yellin' Kid.

"We could if they'd fight fair and even, maybe," assented Bud. "But they'll be on the lookout for trouble, now, and they'll have a big gang of Greasers with them. And while, ordinarily, one cowboy is a match for half a dozen of the ornery Mexicans, you've got to be on the watch for treachery. There's no use tackling this thing unless we have a big enough crowd to meet the biggest bunch Del Pinzo can muster."

"Well, there's some sense in that," admitted Snake. "I'm not afraid of any bunch of rustlers that Hank Fisher can scare up," he went on, "but it isn't a man's personal feelings we got to consider. It's for the good of this ranch. And, as Bud says, we want to make a clean-up this inning."

"That's why I'm going to have help," Bud remarked, as he went to call his father on the telephone.

Mr. Merkel whistled when he heard the disastrous news.

"I didn't think they'd go at it wholesale, that way, Bud," he told his son over the wire. "But you've got the right idea. Go after 'em and clean 'em up! When you take the trail don't turn back until you've finished the job. I'll send you as many men as I can spare, Slim Degnan with 'em!"

"Slim? That's good!" cried Bud. "Now we'll make a clean up. But don't get worried, Dad, if you don't hear from us in several days, or a couple of weeks. We'll probably be out of the reach of a telephone."

"Yes, I realize that! Well, good luck to you. When you going to start?"

"First thing in the morning. Old Billee was shot up a little, so I'll leave him and Buck Tooth to look after what cattle we have left. Can Slim and the others get here in time to start in the morning?"

"They can if I send them over in the jitney which will be quicker, and save them some hard riding. Have you got ponies enough for them?"

"Yes, plenty. Get 'em over here in the gasolene gig and we'll do the rest!" laughed Bud, though he was in anything but a laughing mood, His mind was grimly set on getting back his cattle, and in punishing the evil gang of rustlers that was dominating that section of the "cow country," as ranch localities are sometimes called.

Immediately on hanging up the receiver, Bud Merkel started in on a busy time. Nor were his cousins less engaged. Once the boy ranchers bad determined to "hit the trail," they planned to "do the trick up brown," as

Nort expressed it.

Bud proved himself to be well fitted for the task in hand, in spite of his youth. But he had been well trained by his father, and life on Diamond X had put him in trim for hard fighting. It was not the first time he had had to do with cattle raids, though it was his own first experience on a large scale, and he was vitally interested. He followed the plans he had seen his father put into operation more than once.

Saddles, girths and lariats were looked to, as were all the various trappings of the ponies, without which the raid could not be undertaken in that country of far distances. Then it was necessary to pack sufficient "grub" to last for at least a week, in case no provisions could be come upon.

As for shelter, each man, and by that term I also include the boy ranchers, had a pair of blankets and a tarpaulin to spread under him on the ground. The days were hot, but the nights were cool in spite of camp fires.

Of course each one "packed a gun," some of the cowboys two, and there was no lack of ammunition.

Old Billee felt badly at not being able to go. But his wound was giving him more pain than he liked to admit, and after vainly protesting that he simply must go, he agreed that perhaps it was best for him to remain behind.

In the "jitney," as Mr. Merkel dubbed his auto, several cowboys from Diamond X (including the veteran foreman Slim) reached Happy Valley in due season.

They were fitted out with ponies, and after the situation had been talked over, and every precaution against failure taken, they were ready to start early on the morning following the big raid.

The outfit of the boy ranchers had been sadly depleted by the descent of the unscrupulous gang, and what cattle remained had been driven to the feeding grounds in the vicinity of the reservoir, where Buck Tooth, Old Billee and one man from Diamond X could watch over them.

"Are we all ready?" asked Bud, as he and his cousins, followed in example by the older cowboys vaulted to saddles.

"I reckon so," announced Slim, as he slewed around his holster with its newly-oiled .45.

"Let's go!" said Bud, briefly, and away they started.

They made trail, first, to the scene of the raid. As Bud and the others had anticipated, there were plenty of signs showing where the cattle had been driven off. A large herd was missing, and it must have taken a number of rustlers to have rounded them up and started them toward Double Z, or whatever place was to be used to change, or blur the brands, so the cattle could be sold to some innocent purchaser, perhaps. Though there were not wanting, in that country, not-so-innocent-purchasers of rustled cattle.

"They'll have to keep near grass and water," said Slim, as he rode along with Bud and his cousins. "So we'll do the same."

"Yes, they can't make a dry drive very far," Bud agreed. "They followed this range, it seems."

On reaching the scene of the raid the trail led off to the left, along a tow mountain range or wild and rugged peaks, some, evidently, of volcanic origin. At the foot of this range was grass in plenty, and, occasionally, a water hole, made possible by the fact that End's father had brought the waters of the Pocut River to the valley by means of the tunnel flume.

"The trail's plain enough for a blind man to follow," said Yellin' Kid, who rode beside Snake.

"But it's going to get harder in a little while," spoke Snake. "We're getting into wilder country, and rocks don't take much of an impression. See, it's peterin' out now."

He pointed to the surface of the ground over which they were then traveling. The grass and earth were more and more scanty, and in some places there were patches of shale and rock, on which even an iron-shod hoof would leave no mark.

"Yes, it's a wild country," agreed Bud. "I've never been over as far as this, and I don't believe our cattle ever get here. There isn't enough feed," he added, as he looked around.

The cavalcade was now in a sort of narrow gorge, or gully, with rocky walls on either side, and only scant vegetation on the bottom, where some bunch grass grew. The water seemed to have disappeared.

"They can't drive cattle on a trail like this very far,"

said Slim, looking about with critical eyes.

"And yet they did come in this gulch," said Bud, for the "signs" were still plain.

"Oh, yes, they've been here," agreed Slim. "It sure is a queer trail they picked. I don't see - "

He did not finish the sentence. Somewhere In that lonely and wild section of Happy Valley a single shot rang out, making the echoes vibrate loudly, and awakening a distant coyote, who sent up a mournful howl.

CHAPTER XVIII

THE BOILING SPRING

"What's that?" asked Bud suddenly, his voice seeming almost as loud as that of Yellin' Kid's. The horses had been reined to a halt as soon as the shot sounded, and there was stillness which made the boy rancher's exclamation appear more vociferous than would otherwise have been the case. "What's that?" asked Bud again.

"Some one fired," answered Nort.

"Brilliant!" chuckled Dick. "Bright answer!"

"Almost as bright as my question," conceded Bud, who was willing to admit when he had "pulled a bloomer," as some Englishmen might term it. "It was a shot, though," he added. "I wonder if we'll hear any more?"

They all paused, in listening attitudes; the boy ranchers, the cowboys associated with them in the Happy Valley venture and the others sent with Slim to help run down the rustlers, on whose trail they now were.

But no further firing followed in the three or four minutes they waited there in that lonely gorge, the only sounds being those caused by the restless movements of the steeds.

"I wonder if some one shot at us, or if that was a signal!" remarked Nort, as Bud gave the sign to advance.

"I didn't hear any bullet singin' out this way," drawled Slim. "Not that I'm hankerin' to," he quickly added.

"Then it might have been a signal," went on Nort.

"What makes you say that?" Bud questioned.

"Because it would seem that if the rustlers are ahead of us, trying their best to get far enough away, or to get to some secret hiding place, that they might leave some behind, on the trail, to give warning when we show up," went on Nort.

"Yes, that might be so," slowly admitted Bud. "In fact I think it was, probably, a signal, and it may have been given by the same one who gave signals before."

"What do you mean?" asked Dick.

"I mean Four Eyes, and the lantern flashes we saw from the watch tower that night we rode in," Bud answered. "I believe Four Eyes was and still is, in with the rustlers, and that he gave a signal to show that everything was ready for the raid."

"But the raid didn't take place until some time after we saw those flashing lights," said Dick.

"It takes some time to get a cattle-rustling gang

together," declared Bud. "I wish we could find Four Eyes."

His gaze roved the sides of the lonely gorge, and sought to pierce the maze of the trail ahead. But as it wound in and out, following the windings of the defile, he could not see far in that direction.

"If it was Four Eyes, he played his game mighty slick!" declared Yellin' Kid. "He fooled us all, includin' your paw, Bud!"

"Well, if we get on his trail, and can connect him with the rustlers, which it won't be hard to do, I'm thinking, he won't play any more tricks," declared the western lad vindictively and with righteous anger. "But if that was a warning shot, and that's what it seems it must have been, we'd better take some precautions ourselves."

"Such as what-like?" asked Slim, willing to let Bud take the lead, as the search for the rustlers was distinctly an affair of the boy ranchers.

"We ought not to go ahead, all in a bunch," decided Bud. "We may run into a bunch of Greasers at some turn of the trail, and if we have scouts out we can handle the situation better."

"I was going to suggest it," said Slim, "but I thought you'd think of it yourself, Bud, being as you're your paw's son."

Bud was pleased at the implied compliment, and, a little later, as they advanced, they were divided into three small parties, with rear and vanguard, to insure against a surprise in back, which might easily happen.

And so they advanced through the defile, keeping watch on both sides of the trail. There were still evidences that a herd of cattle had been driven along the rocky defile, but because of the rocky floor, if such it may be called, the signs were faint, and only an experienced westerner could have picked them up. But the boy ranchers were accompanied by experienced cow punchers, who knew every trick of the trail.

Bud had insisted that it was one of his rights to ride in the advance guard, with Yellin' Kid, and it was while they were performing this duty, of watching for a surprise, that they saw, just around the bend of the trail, some wisps of white vapor floating up.

"There they are!" exclaimed Bud in a hoarse whisper, pointing. "They've stopped there - or some of 'em have. Or maybe it's the person who fired the warning shot."

"Might be," admitted Yellin' Kid, toning his voice down somewhat to suit the occasion. "Better let me get off and crawl ahead, Bud. I'm used to that. You hold the horses."

Bud realized the sense of this proposition, and he held the reins of the Kid's horse, while that cow puncher slipped from the saddle, and, on all fours, crept toward the wall of rock which rose abruptly at a turn of the trail shutting off a view beyond.

Bud watched Yellin' Kid closely, the lad's hand on the butt of his .45, and occasionally he glanced back to catch the first glimpse of the main party, so he might warn them. He saw the wisps of vapor rising and floating toward him.

"Not much smoke," mused Bud. "They're using very dry wood - regular Indian trick. I wonder -"

A moment later he heard Yellin' Kid shout, and it was such a cry as indicated pain. Yet Bud had heard no shot.

"I wonder if they knifed him?" was the thought that flashed into Bud's brain. He cast caution to the winds and galloped forward, making a great racket, and casting loose the reins of the Kid's steed.

The sight that met Bud's eyes was enough to startle him, though it was not what he expected to see.

For he beheld Yellin' Kid standing in front of a pillar of white vapor, or, rather, the cowboy was dancing about, holding one hand in the other, and using excited slang at a rate that soon would exhaust his vocabulary, Bud thought.

But, more strange than anything else, was the fact that there was no sign of a fire, to cause the white vapor, nor was there any indication that anyone besides Yellin' Kid and Bud were in the immediate neighborhood. No rustlers had started the blaze which caused the white clouds to drift upward.

"What's the matter, Kid?" asked Bud, as he saw that something had happened. "Where's the fire?"

"Under there!" and the cowboy pointed to the ground. "Keep away from it. Don't go near that spring, an' whatever you do, don't put your hand in. I did, an' I'm sorry for it!"

"Spring! Fire! What is it, anyhow!" asked Bud, as he slid from the saddle and ran forward.

"It's a boilin' spring, that's what it is!" declared Yellin' Kid. "Boilin' hot an' it near took th' skin from my hand! What you see is steam - not smoke! Horned toads and hoop-skirts! It's as hot as Buck Tooth's tea kettle! Look out for the boilin' spring!"

CHAPTER XIX

IN A MAZE

Bud stood in amazement looking at Kid and listening to what the excited cowboy was saying. Then the gaze of the western boy rancher turned toward a depression in the ground, whence arose what he and Yellin' Kid had thought was smoke but which, in reality, was steam from a hot spring.

"A boiler, eh?" repeated Bud. "First I ever knew we had any so near Happy Valley."

"Me, either," went on Kid. "I suspicioned what it was when I got close and couldn't smell any wood burnin'. Then I put my hand out, but the steam fooled me. I didn't know the top of the water was so close, an' I dipped right down into it. Whew! It was hot!"

"Did it scald you?" asked Bud.

"Pretty nigh it," answered the cowboy, exhibiting a very red hand.

At this moment a noise behind the two attracted their attention. They turned to see pointed at them the black openings of two .45 guns, and they had glimpses of eager eyes looking over the sights of the weapons.

"Don't shoot! I'll come down!" laughed Bud, in imitation of what was the current saying concerning the famous Davy Crockett.

"What is it?" asked Nort, owner of one of the menacing guns, as he arose and slid his .45 into the holster.

"Did they get away?" Dick wanted to know, as he stood beside his brother. The two boys had left the main body and worked their way up to join the vanguard, in the persons of Bud and Kid.

"There wasn't anyone to get away," Bud answered grimly. "It was only a boiling spring, and we took the steam of it for smoke."

"Boiling spring!" cried Nort. "I never saw one before."

"Me, either," added his brother, and together they looked at the depression in the ground, filled with scalding hot water. At times it bubbled up, like some great kettle over a fire, and then the steam was as thick as the smoke at some camp fire when green wood is used. Again the spring was comparatively quiet.

"I've seen 'em before," remarked Bud, "though I didn't know we had any so near Happy Valley. There's lots of 'em out in the Yellowstone Park region, and in other places, some not many miles from here."

"Any volcanoes?" asked Nort.

"Or geysers?" Dick queried.

"Not that I know of," Bud answered. "You don't need

volcanoes to make boiling springs, though I suppose the hot water must be boiled over some internal fire beneath the earth's surface. And these same fires do, sometimes, make volcanoes.

"But I've never seen any volcanoes around here; have you, fellows?" and he appealed to the cowboys.

"Not since I came up from Mexico," one answered. "I was close to one there. And I've seen Old Faithful, and some of the other geysers in the Yellowstone."

"They put soap in some to make 'em spout, don't they?" asked Dick, who remembered to have read something to that effect.

"So I've heard," the cowboy said, "though it isn't supposed to be done. It sort of wears out the geyser, I believe, though I don't know much about such things. Anyhow, I don't know of any around here, though I have seen a few boiling springs, farther to the south."

"Yes, I have, too," Bud admitted. "Well, here's one, and she sure is hot," he added, as a sudden activity on the part of the phenomenon sent up another cloud of steam. "We could boil eggs there if we had any."

"We brought some along," Dick said, "but they're hard-boiled already. No use doing the job over. Say, but this is interesting!" he added, as the spring suddenly spouted up a little way, almost like a miniature geyser.

"It would be more interesting if we could get closer on the trail of that gang of cattle thieves, and take away our steers," said Bud. "I wonder if the poor animals hurried in here for water, and couldn't drink it because it was hot?" He recalled days of helping haze cattle on long trails, when the creatures were tormented by thirst, and he knew how they suffered.

"There are a few signs that they've been in here," remarked Slim, as the party was gathered around the boiling spring. "But they aren't here now."

"Not much use in us staying here, either," commented Bud, as he looked around on the bleak and cheerless prospect. Except for the boiling spring there was no sign of natural life. All about were great and small rocks, piles of shale and jagged stones, as though the place had been swept by a prehistoric fire. They were in one of the twists and turns of the rocky defile, and it was a rocky pass, with no trees or grass growing except near the top, and these appeared to be a sort of overgrowth from the grass and foliage growing down above.

"No, they didn't stop here long," declared Yellin' Kid. "They passed on, an' that's what we got to do."

"Might as well stay here and have grub, now we're dismounted," suggested Nort.

The idea was voted a good one, and was soon put into operation. They ate and talked of what had passed and what lay before them. Of the latter they could only conjecture, but it is safe to say that not one of them in his wildest imagination ever conjectured such an ending to their trailing as actually occurred.

"Well, let's get on," called Bud, when appetites had been satisfied - that is all but those of the horses. There was no grass for them, though they did manage to drink some of the water from the boiling spring where it had collected in little pools, and had cooled. But this would never have sufficed for hundreds of cattle.

Once more they were on the way, and shortly afterward they left the grim and rocky defile for a more fertile region, where there was grass for the animals. But they were still down between a range of high hills which towered on either side.

The trail twisted and turned, this way and that, winding back and forth. But ever there was to be seen, here and there, signs that the herd of cattle had been driven this way. Faint the signs were, at times, and at last they disappeared altogether.

"Where have they gone?" asked Nort.

"Looks like they dropped down a hole, but there isn't any hole here," said Yellin' Kid.

"Oh, we'll pick the trail up later on," suggested Bud.

But even as they started off once more Bud, who had just consulted a compass he carried, uttered a cry of amazement.

"What's the matter?" asked Slim.

"We're going the wrong way," declared Bud. "We're heading north instead of south. We're all turned around! Something's wrong!"

CHAPTER XX

A SURPRISE

Some of those in the rear, who had heard Bud's exclamation, but who had not clearly heard what he said, came crowding up. Among them was Snake Purdee, and his eyes sparkled with hidden emotion as he inquired:

"Did you see any rattlers? This is just the place for 'em!"

"Yes, we came acrost a nest of baby ones what had lost their mother, an' they're countin' on you t' bring 'em up on th' bottle!" laughed Slim. The men, more or less, poked fun at Snake because of his great fear of reptiles, and Slim could not forego this chance.

But Snake understood the game, and realized that he had nothing to fear. He shot a look at Slim, however, which indicated that there would be an attempt, later, to get even.

"What's wrong?" asked Slim, for in his endeavor to play a joke on Snake he had not paid much attention to what Bud was saying.

"We're all turned around," spoke the western lad. "All

in a maze. We started out, heading south, and we've kept, generally, to that direction ever since. But now we're heading back north. Looks like we'd lost the trail."

Slim and some of the more experienced cowboys studied the trail for several minutes. Surely it did seem to "peter out," as Yellin' Kid expressed it, though it had been fairly plain up to this point.

"They couldn't get up on either side," declared Nort, looking at the steep, rocky walls which hemmed the trailers in right and left.

"And they haven't gone on ahead, for there isn't a sign," added Dick, who had ridden up the defile for some little distance, returning to make his report. "Nothing short of an air ship could have lifted up a bunch of cattle from this gorge and set 'em down farther on."

"Unless they went through a hole in one of the side walls," suggested Slim, "like that underground river you fellows discovered in the tunnel."

"There are no side passages here," declared Bud. And he seemed to hold the correct view of it, the others agreeing, after a careful inspection of the rocky and shale-covered walls on either hand. "It looks just as if they came up to this point and - vanished!"

"Pretty slick work - I'll give Del Pinzo credit for that," said Slim, as if it were already established that the wily Greaser halfbreed had made the descent on Happy Valley. "How he and his bunch could haze cattle this far into a rocky pass, an' then make 'em disappear, gets me!"

"It shore do!" shouted Yellin' Kid.

"But that doesn't change the fact that we're all switched around," declared Bud. "We're going north instead of south!"

"Not so hard to account for that," said Snake. "This vale just naturally twists and turns like a windin' river. I wouldn't wonder but what we'd been going north other times, only you never noticed your compass, Bud."

"Well, maybe so," admitted the boy rancher, rather dubiously. "But it looks as if we were back-trailing, instead of keeping on after those rascals."

"We're keeping on all right!" asserted Slim. "By some hook or crook they've fooled us, but we haven't passed 'em, that's certain, and they must be somewhere up ahead. It would take Rocky Mountain goats to scramble up thcrc," he added, motioning toward the steep walls of the gorge. "Some trick ponies might do it, but no cattle ever could, unless they're like some of them Swiss cheese brand I seen in pictures!"

"Then do you think we should keep on?" asked Dick.

"I shore do!" declared the foreman.

"Forward march!" cried Bud, with a little laugh. "We want to get our cattle back, and catch the rustlers who took 'em!"

And so, though all signs of the trail seemed to have

vanished, they kept on. Night saw them in even a wilder region, though there was a spring of water - not boiling this time - and some grass for the animals. So it was decided to camp there and take up the search in the morning.

They were in the enemy's country in every sense of the word, and could afford to take no chances. So after a fire had been built, and coffee made, bacon and flapjacks being the other items on the bill of fare, the men and boys were told off into watches.

Bud and Slim, Nort and Snake, and Dick and Yellin' Kid were assigned to divide the night among them working as partners in the order named. The others were to be allowed to roll up and get what sleep they could, Bud and Slim taking the first watch.

That passed off uneventfully, as did the vigil of Nort and Snake, nothing more important occurring than the distant howls of the coyotes.

When it was the turn of Dick and Yellin' Kid they rolled out, albeit sleepy and tired, to stand guard until morning, when the trail would again be taken up.

"Zimmy! But it's chilly!" said Kid in a low voice, as lie tossed some wood on the fire and wrapped his blanket more closely about him.

"Yes, it always is just before sunrise," added Dick. "I wonder what we'll find after daylight?"

"I hope we find that ornery bunch!" murmured Yellin' Kid, keeping down his voice so as not to awaken the sleepers.

"So do I," said Dick.

Then they sat about the fire, occasionally strolling around the improvised camp, to make sure that none of their enemies were creeping up on them in the darkness.

The stars shone clear and bright in the sky above, and occasionally a little wind swept up the dismal defile. Now and then a loose stone rattled down the sides of shale and volcanic rock, and at such times Dick, and even Yellin' Kid started, and felt for their guns. But all the alarms were false ones.

That is, the watchers decided they were, for no sight was had of anyone until Dick, after a stroll about the fire, suddenly started back and whispered to Yellin' Kid:

"Isn't that a head looking up over that rock?"

The Kid glanced to where Dick directed his gaze, and, in an instant, the cowboy had his weapon out and leveled. His finger was even pressing the trigger when he laughed silently and thrust the .45 back in its leather case. "Why didn't you shoot?" asked Dick.

"It was an owl," answered Kid. "It was his ears you seen stickin' up! Listen!"

And, a moment later, there was the mournful hooting of the nocturnal bird, which had flown away, but on such downy-feathered wings that it made no sound.

"An owl!" murmured Dick. Then he was glad he had not shot first, as he had intended. He would only have awakened the others and been laughed at for his pains. Sometimes, he reflected, it was better to hold your fire, even in the west, that region of quick action.

Soon there was a little grayish, pinkish light to be observed over the edge of the eastern hill. It grew slowly, and daylight came, though it was some time before the sun itself was seen, so deep were the searchers down in the defile.

After breakfast they set out again, looking carefully for signs of the rustlers, but they saw none, and at last they decided that, in some mysterious manner, their quarry had given them the slip.

"Though I don't see how they did it," declared Slim, somewhat vexed that he and his men were not better able to pick up the trail.

"There must be some side passage - like that!" suddenly declared Yellin' Kid, leaping from his horse and then, as suddenly disappearing from the sight of his companions. "Hey! What's the idea! Where'd he go?" asked Snake.

"In this side passage," answered Yellin' Kid, as suddenly reappearing. "Look, here's a crack, or fissure in the rock, I saw it from where I sat on my pony. It goes off from th' main trail, but I can't see where it leads."

They all dismounted and investigated. As the Kid had said, it was a traverse defile, opening out of the main one and almost at right angles. The opening was concealed behind a great pinnacle of rock, so that the cleft was only visible from a certain point, and it was at this point that the Kid saw it.

"Where does it go to?" asked Bud as they entered, single file. It was only wide enough for that.

"We've got to follow and see!" said Slim.

"If there was a place like that, back where we discovered we were in a maze, it would have been easy enough for the rustlers to have driven the cattle through, one at a time," observed Nort.

"But there wasn't any such place!" declared Bud. "We made sure of that. But where does this lead?"

That was what they all conjectured, and they were soon to learn. As they rode along, the side cleft widened, until there was room enough for three to ride abreast. And it was while thus progressing that Dick, who was in the lead with Slim and Snake, made a surprising discovery. He rode around a turn in the new trail, and at the sight of something beyond, in the smaller, rocky defile, he set up such a shout as brought all his companions to his side.

"What is it?" shouted Bud.

"Look!" answered Dick, pointing. "Del Pinzo and big gang!"

CHAPTER XXI

IN PURSUIT

Two deep-throated shouts echoed amid the winding mazes of the small canyon leading off from the main gulch that the boy ranchers and their friends had been following. One shout followed closely on that of Dick, announcing his amazing discovery. The other came from the band of rascals whose hiding place had at last been spied out, and by a mere chance at that.

One shout was that of joyful anticipation, and this came from Bud, Dick, Nort and the friends from Diamond X. This shout had in it an anticipation of righteous punishment to be inflicted on those who had stolen the cattle.

The other shout was of baffled rage that their hiding place had been discovered. This shout came from Del Pinzo and his gang.

For it was the lawless Mexican half-breed and his followers, numbering in all more than two score, whom Dick had seen as he made the turn in that winding and narrow gorge. At a place where the rocky defile flared out, making a sort of amphitheatre there were gathered about a spring of water, their horses tethered where they could crop the scanty herbage, the crowd of which our friends had long been in pursuit.

Following the two shouts - one of pleased discovery and the other of baffled rage at being discovered - there was quick action.

"Here they are!" shouted Bud, as soon as he had joined Dick, and had seen what the latter had fairly stumbled upon. "Here's the Del Pinzo crowd!"

Up came riding Nort, Slim, Snake and the others.

"Oh, boy! We've got 'em just where we want 'em," was the exclamation of Yellin' Kid. And I leave you to judge in what tone he uttered the words.

"Unlimber, boys!" called Slim Degnan, grimly and significantly as he whipped out his .45. "There's likely to be action!"

"Hold on! Wait a minute!" counseled Snake, as Bud and his cousins were about to urge their horses forward. The cowboy reached out, and his hand fell with a firm grip on the bridle of Bud's steed.

"What's the idea?" asked that boy rancher. "Now we've found the rascals, can't we go in and clean 'em up?"

"That's natural Bud, most natural," conceded Snake. "But what's th' use runnin' your head in a bee's nest if yon can git th' honey some other way?"

"You mean it won't be safe to ride up to 'em and fight 'em?'?" asked Nort.

"Somethin' like that, yes, son," answered the cowboy.

"I think Del Pinzo an' his crowd have been waitin' for just such a chance as this. They'd ask nothin' better than t' have us rush 'em, an' then they'd have a good excuse for sayin', afterward, that they popped us off in self-defense."

"Snake's right!" declared Yellin' Kid, modulating his voice somewhat. "We'd better play this hand cautious like."

Seeing that this was the sentiment of the more experienced men, Bud and his cousins held back, and a moment later, urged by the cowboys, the ranch lads had turned aside and the whole body of pursuers had retreated to a position somewhat away from the turn of the trail where Dick had looked through the defile and had seen the rascals encamped.

"What's the next move?" asked Nort, as the party gathered together, giving their horses a breathing spell, for which the animals were, doubtless, very thankful.

"We'd better look for some shelter," advised Snake, "an' then see what we can do toward learnin' th' intentions of this bunch of bad actors."

"You mean sort of spy 'em out?" asked Dick.

"That's it," chimed in Yellin' Kid. "If this is goin' to be a fight, an' it shore looks as if there was, we want to take all th' advantage we can. They outnumber us two to one!"

This was true enough. The fleeting glimpse our friends had of the outlaws, through the crack in the rocky wall, showed that there were more than two score under the leadership of the unscrupulous Del Pinzo.

Following the skilful advice of the cowboys, Bud and his cousins took their places behind some sheltering rocks, leading their horses in with them, for much depended on their mounts. Without them it meant giving up the chase. And even if one pony was killed or wounded, it meant that its owner would have to make his way back on foot, which was neither pleasant nor safe.

"Get your guns ready," said Slim. "There's going to be action, but not just yet. We want this to be a winnin' fight if we can make it so."

Once within comparative shelter, and feeling somewhat calmer after the first wild excitement, Bud, Nort and Dick looked to their older companions for further advice.

"Somebody's got t' go back t' that crack, unbeknownst t' them scoundrels, an' see what they're doin'," decided Slim.

"S'pose they're there yet?" asked Bud.

"Either that, or they've taken the alarm an' are on their way, or they're doin' just what we are - gittin' ready for a fight," said the foreman grimly. "An' what it is they're doin' we want t' know. Snake, you're pretty good at Indian tactics. S'pose you sneak up there an' take a look in."

"All right," was the ready answer.

Of course Bud, Nort and Dick, each and every one of

them, wished they had been selected for this duty. But while they were rapidly learning the ways of the west, in dealing with desperate characters, it was better at this time to have an experienced man spy out the movements of Del Pinzo and his gang. This Snake set out to do.

"An' while he's gone, th' rest of us want t' sort of make up our minds what t' do," said Slim. "If that bunch is gettin' ready t'rush us, same as we may be able to do on our own hook, we want t' have some plan of action."

So a sort of council of war was held, during the absence of Snake, who was soon lost to sight among the rocks, the cowboy making his way in a crouching, crawling position that almost resembled the reptiles he so feared and hated.

There was some low-voiced talk among the remaining cowboys, in which talk Bud and his cousins had no part. For a moment the lads feared there was some scheme afoot to put them in places of safety, out of danger so to speak. And the boy ranchers weren't going tamely to submit to this.

"I say, Slim," exclaimed Bud, with this fear in mind, "we are going to do our share in this fighting, you know!"

"Shore I know it!" grunted the foreman. "You'll have all th' scrappin' you want, if these fellows don't vamoose without firin' a shot! We was just talkin' of the best place t' put you."

"Oh," murmured Bud, "all right."

Willard F. Baker

After some little talk, and a survey of the ground to which the pursuers had retreated in order to make a temporary stand, each person's position was designated, and then guns were loosed in holsters and the supply of cartridges was looked to.

"As soon as Snake comes back we'll know what t' do," Slim said.

"He ought to be along soon now," remarked Dick.

Hardly had he spoken than there was a noise among the loose rocks and boulders some distance up the gulch - in the direction the spying-out cowboy had taken.

"Here he comes!" exclaimed Bud, and his hand went to his gun, for it was very possible that Snake would be pursued, and have to retreat on the run.

However the alarm proved to be a false one, for, after waiting some time, Snake not having appeared, it was surmised that some rock had become loose and rolled down the steep side of the gulch.

The waiters and watchers were just beginning to get a bit worried, and Bud was on the point of suggesting that he be allowed to go look for Snake, when the cowboy came back.

So quietly did he approach, and so unexpected was his appearance that Nort and Dick, on whose side of the improvised "fort" Snake first showed himself, were startled.

"If that had been any of the Del Pinzo crowd they'd

have been on top of us before we knew it," confessed Nort.

"Not much!" laughed Bud. "Slim has seen Snake coming along this last three minutes; haven't you, Slim?"

"Yep! I noticed him, but I didn't say anythin'," acknowledged the foreman. "I seen that he was alone. But what's the verdict, Snake?" he asked, anxiously. "Are they gittin' ready t' come at us here, or are they leavin'?"

"Neither one," was the answer, "but they're gettin' ready to do suthin! They're all in a bunch in the middle of that place, holdin' a confab, I reckon. It's hard to say what they are up to. But I got a hunch that if we rushed 'em we could throw a scare int' 'em, anyhow."

"Do you think they know we're here?" asked Bud.

"Oh, sure!" was the answer. "At least they saw us an' heard us when we reached that crack. But of course they can only guess what we're up to now, when we didn't rush 'em first shot. They might have known, though, what our plans was, if I hadn't cracked their spy on the head!" said Snake, calmly.

"You did what?" asked Slim.

"Just as I got t' th' place where I could look in," went on the cowboy, "I saw one of them Greasers up t' the same trick I was tryin' to pull off. He was sneakin' down this way, but I saw him first. Caught a glimpse of his head around the edge of a rock; I just reached out with my gun and tapped him on the noodle."

"Kill him?" asked Dick.

"No. Guess not. Just stretched him out so he can't go back an' tell any tales for a time. Now the way I figger it is this: They'll be waitin' for a report on what their spy sees, same as you was waitin' for me t' come back. Only their spy won't show up for a couple o' hours, an' that gives us a chance to act."

"What had we better do?" asked Yellin' Kid.

"Rush 'em!" instantly decided Snake. "Let's git t' that openin' as quiet as we can, an' rush right for 'em! This rest has freshened our horses, an' we're in better shape now."

"Not so much so, as far as horses go," dubiously declared Slim. "They're pretty badly spent, and can't do much racin'. But I guess maybe it is better for us t' get into action, instid of waitin' for that bunch t' come here. As Snake says, they'll be lookin' for their spy t' come back, an' maybe we can take 'em unawares."

So, after some further talk, it was decided to mount again, ride to the opening that led from the main trail into the hiding place of the outlaws, and boldly attack them.

True, our friends were outnumbered, but they had right on their side, and this sometimes makes a difference. Also they would have a little advantage, they hoped, in making the attack somewhat unexpectedly. For though Del Pinzo and his crowd knew the ranchmen were in the neighborhood they would, as Snake believed, await the return of the spy they had sent out, before doing anything.

"An' that spy won't come t' his senses very soon," declared the avenging cowboy. "When he does he'll have an awful headache!"

As quietly as possible they made their way to the opening. Slim, as a sort of captain, was in advance of the others and looked in. He came back to say:

"They're gettin' ready for suthin'! They're all standin' near their horses, an' seem to be plannin' a move. Get ready t' rush in when I give the word!"

There was a final look to arms and saddle leathers, and then the foreman cried:

"Get into action!" at the same time spurring forward his pony, an example followed by all the others as they rushed into the defile.

And action there was, but not exactly of the kind the boy ranchers and their friends anticipated. For Del Pinzo (easily recognized among the lesser lights of rascaldom) with his followers, after their first angry shouts, leaped for their horses. And their agility in that respect spoke well for their preparedness. In an instant, it seemed, every one of the two score, and more, was in saddle, and headed out of the defile. They were retreating - riding away from the following avengers, and going, it seemed, further into the maze of winding clefts amid the mountains.

To the credit of Del Pinzo - if credit it be and if he be entitled to get credit - he rode at the rear, not starting his horse until all his men had raced away ahead of him.

And then, as Bud, Dick and the others pressed into the defile after them, the Greaser turned and fired once, but with such quick action that eye could scarce follow the motion of his hand and weapon.

There was a sharp crack and the hat of Yellin' Kid, who rode immediately behind Bud, sailed off his head, at the same time that a bullet zipped viciously over the pursuers.

"Close call that, Kid!" remarked Snake, leaning over as his horse galloped forward, and picking up his friend's hat.

"Close nothin'!" snapped out Yellin' Kid. "That was fancy shootin'! If Del Pinzo wanted to get me he could 'a' done it. He can mark out th' pips on a ten spot card with his eyes shut, almost! He shot my hat off just to show he wasn't aimin' t' spill no innocent blood! But wait until I get him! I'll make him sweat for that! A hole through brim an' crown! Why couldn't he be decent about it an' make it one?" grumbled Yellin' Kid as Snake handed him the hat.

"Never mind that!" shouted Slim Degnan. "If we're going t' get them fellers we got t' ride!"

That was evident, for even as he spoke Del Pinzo, the last of the outlaws, disappeared around a turn in the defile. He was "hazing" his men along to some other hiding place, it appeared. And he and his rascally followers seemed to know their ground, for they rode at break-neck pace, without fear of what lay beyond and unseen. It is likely they had traveled that route before.

Another advantage lay with the rustlers. Their horses were fresh, for from the negligent attitudes assumed by the men when Dick had discovered them, it was evident they had been at ease for some time, whereas the pursuers had been on the trail a long time, and the way had been rough and stony.

So it is nothing to the discredit of the boy ranchers that they and their friends were distanced in the first wild rush following the discovery and alarm.

"Come on!" cried Bud. "Come on!" and he and Dick for the moment were in the lead, the canyon being wide enough, here, for several to ride abreast. "We've got to get 'em!"

"And we won't stop until we do!" added his cousin.

But they reckoned not with the roughness of the way, the start the rustlers had, their fresher horses and the fact that Del Pinzo and his crowd were more familiar with the trail than were the boy ranchers. So though our heroes rode on as fast as they could go with comparative safety, they did not, for some time at least, again come within sight of the enemy.

"Wait there! Hold on a little!" finally called Slim to Bud, Dick and Nort, who, in their youthful and natural eagerness, had forged to the front in a bunch. "Pull up! This isn't a hundred yard dash! It's going to be a long race!"

Bud was beginning to believe this, and some of his first exuberance was disappearing. He was getting more cool-headed.

Willard F. Baker

"Let's take it a bit easy," he said to Nort and Dick. "I guess we've got a long trail to follow."

"But we've got to get 'em!" declared Dick.

"You got rid of something that time!" commented his brother, meaningly, if slangily. "We're going to make 'em give back our cattle!"

"Say!" suddenly cried Bud. "That's the queer part of it! Where are the steers?"

And for the first time it occurred to the minds of the boy ranchers that of that quarry they had come most in search of they had had not a glimpse. Not a steer was in sight!

Something of the amazement they felt must have been depicted on their faces, for when Slim rode up to where the boy ranchers had halted he asked:

"What's the matter?"

"Where are the cattle?" asked Bud, shouting almost as loudly as Yellin' Kid would have done. "Did you notice they didn't have a one with them, Slim?"

"Yes. Are you just waking up to that, Bud?"

"I reckon I am. But what does it mean?"

"It means that there's a deeper game being played than we have any idea of, son. We've got to go some to get to the bottom!"

CHAPTER XXII

BUD'S DISCOVERY

Once it became evident that catching the rustlers was likely to be the work of a long chase on the trail, the whole party of pursuers came to a halt beside the boy ranchers. And after some rapid talk of what might lay beyond their stopping place, in a lonely, wild and desolate section of the defile, the conversation switched to what had surprised Bud and his cousins - the absence of the cattle.

"I s'posed they were driving the steers ahead of 'em all along," admitted North "They drove the animals off our ranch, and I didn't think but what they were hazing 'em along to some place where they could change or blur the brands, and then sell 'em."

"That's what I thought, too," acknowledged Dick.

"Well, I must say I didn't think much about it," confessed Bud. "When I saw Del Pinzo and his gang in there all I wanted to do was to come to hand-grips with 'em. I forgot all about the cattle. But after we'd chased along a bit I did begin to wonder where my animals were - *our* animals, I should say," he corrected himself with a glance at his cousins. However, they understood.

"They must have gotten the cattle over to Double Z, or wherever it is they dispose of 'em," suggested Dick.

"They couldn't - not in this short time," declared Slim. "We followed 'em too close. Besides, there isn't a sign of any cattle having been here, nor in that place where we surprised th' head Greaser and his gang. Not a sign of cattle!"

He looked up and down the gorge, as did the other cowboys. But not even the sharpest eye could detect the faintest "sign" of the steers having been driven along the passage.

"They must have them hidden somewhere," said Dick. "We'd better go back to the place where the sign petered out. There must be some opening there out of the main canyon."

"If there is it's so well hid that it takes sharper eyes than I've got to find it," declared Snake, and he was noted for his far-seeing and clear vision.

"Go *back*!" exclaimed North impulsively. "We aren't going back, are we, until we get Del Pinzo and his gang?"

"Shoot 'em up - that's what I advise!" cried Yellin' Kid. There was a moment's pause, and Bud spoke.

"We're got two things to do," said the boy rancher. "One is to get our cattle back, and the other is to nab the rustlers. But it's more important to get the cattle, I think.

"If we don't do that our ranch experiment will be a

failure," he went on. "But, of course, for the sake of other ranchers, it would be a mighty good thing if we could put Del Pinzo and his rustler crowd out of business."

"Can't we do both?" asked Nort.

"That's what I was coming to," his cousin continued. "If we can get on the trail of the hidden steers - for hidden they are, I'm sure - we can haze them back to the valley. Then we can keep on after this crowd," and he nodded toward the winding trail that led down the narrow defile.

"Then you think we'd better go back!" asked Dick.

"Let's see what Slim says" answered Bud. Naturally he would turn to his father's foreman for advice.

"Oh, you're leavin' it t' me, are you?" asked Slim, as he finished rolling his cigarette, a feat he could accomplish with one hand. Then he lighted it, took a satisfying puff and went on: "If you ask my advice I'd say to go back an' see if you can't locate the cattle. As Bud remarks, they're dollars an' cents. Th' rustlers aren't, though it would be a mighty good stunt t' wipe 'em off th' face of this cow country. But maybe we can attend to *them* later."

"Turn back she is!" exclaimed Bud, accepting, as did the others, the advice of Slim as being final. "We'll see if we can find the cattle, and then haze them to a safe place. After that we'll nab Del Pinzo and his bunch - if we can," he added, as a saving clause.

"Suits me!" remarked Yellin' Kid, taking off his hat

Willard F. Baker

and looking at the two bullet holes. "That nabbin' part is what I want t' play at," and his grin suggested that when he and the Greaser met there would be some interesting happenings.

It having been thus decided that the pursuit would be abandoned for the time being, a sort of council of war was held to settle on the next course.

"I say grub!" exclaimed Bud, knowing that the suggestion would come with better grace from him than from some of the men who were working for him and his father. "Let's eat!"

There was no debate on this question and when the ponies had been turned loose to graze on what scanty grass they could find, a fire was made and preparations started for feeding the hungry posse. For they were that - both hungry and a posse, bent on the capture of the lawless rustlers. Though, for the time, righteous revenge was given over to the more practical side of the question - getting back the cattle.

Probably you do not need to be told that little time was wasted over the meal, simple as it was. Cowboys, on the trail, or otherwise engaged in their work of the ranch or range, do not spend much time over the pleasures of the appetite. There is a time for feasting, and a time for chasing cattle rustlers, and there was no sense in combining the two. That, evidently, was the thought in the minds of Bud and his friends, for they hurried through their eating, and, having rested the horses, were soon in saddles again.

"Now," remarked Bud, talking the matter over with Slim, "what is the best plan?"

"To get back, as fast as we can, t' th' place where we saw th' last signs of th' cattle," was the foreman's answer. "The unravelin' of th' skein of mystery, t' use a poetical expression, Bud, is there!"

They all agreed with this view of it, and after a short ride down the defile, to see, if by chance, any of the Del Pinzo crowd might be in evidence, or returning, the back trail was taken.

"We aren't going to discover much this day," observed Bud, as he rode slowly along between Nort and Dick.

"Why, did you see a black rabbit?" Nort asked, remembering what had happened when a similar incident occurred, just before the strange events narrated in the chapter preceding this.

"No, I didn't see a black jack," Bud answered. "But it won't be long until dark, for we don't get the full benefit of the afternoon sun down in this gorge. And we can't do anything except by daylight. No use looking for sign in the dark."

"That's right," agreed Nort. "But I was afraid it was a black rabbit you'd seen."

"As if we didn't have enough bad luck without that," commented Dick. "It's as bad, losing your herd as it is not to have enough water to give 'em what they need," and he referred to the time when, by the efforts of this same Del Pinzo, the supply for the reservoir of Happy Valley was cut off.

"Oh, well, it might be worse," observed Bud, with a sort of cheerful, philosophical air, for he was of rather a happy disposition.

"How?" asked Snake, for he was rather "sore" because Del Pinzo and the rustlers had escaped. Perhaps Snake felt that he might have gone in and captured the outlaws single-handed when he was on the lone spying expedition.

"Well, I might never have had any cattle for those fellows to steal," went on Bud. "But say, boys," he went on, as they came to a place where the trail seemed to divide. "Let's take this other road back. It looks a bit easier, and we want to favor the ponies all we can."

"Go ahead," advised Slim, to whom Bud looked for confirmation of his plan. "Anything that makes it easier for th' horses makes it more sure for us. And we may have a long hunt ahead of us."

The care taken by the boy ranchers and their friends of their animals was not exaggerated, nor unusual. In the West so much depends on a man's horse - his comfort and very life, often - that it is a foolish fellow, indeed, who will not bestow at least some thought and care on his horse. The animal becomes a trusted companion and friend to the cowboys and prospectors.

So, in order, as he hoped, to provide an easier means of getting back to the place they wished to reach, Bud led the way along a different trail on the retreat.

It was practically a retreat, though one they had selected for themselves, since the outlaws had distanced them.

It was rather a dejected bunch of boy ranchers and their friends that were now back-trailing. There was not much talk, after the excitement of the attack which had "petered out," and even Bud, gay and cheerful as he usually was, now seemed to have little to say.

It was Dick who startled them all by suddenly exclaiming:

"Look ahead there! Isn't that a man on the trail?" He, with Nort and Bud were in advance of the others. Dick pointed toward the place where he thought he saw something suspicious.

"I don't glimpse anything," observed Nort.

"Nor I," said his cousin.

"He's gone now," Dick stated. "But I did see some one, and I'm almost sure it was a Greaser. Looked just like one of their hats."

"What is it!" called Slim, for he caught snatches of the rather excited talk of the boys.

"Dick thought he saw one of the Del Pinzo gang," answered Bud.

"Maybe he's the fellow I cracked on the head," suggested Snake. For they had lost sight of that individual in the mad rush into the canyon, and had not seen him when they turned back.

"Say, wouldn't it be a good thing to capture him?" asked Bud eagerly. "We could make him tell where the others are, and where our cattle are hidden."

"If we can get him," conceded Slim.

"There he is again!" cried Dick. "Come on, fellows!"

Disregarding, or forgetting the travel-weary horses, the ranch lad urged his own steed ahead at as rapid a pace as the animal could be induced to develop in a spurt.

"Take it easy!" advised Nort to his brother, but he might as well have called to the wind, for Dick was off and away.

"I don't see anything!" cried Bud, and though he had looked eagerly forward at Dick's call he had glimpsed neither hat nor face of any personage who might be suspected of being one of the Del Pinzo gang.

But, even with that, Bud was not going to miss a chance to be in at the finish of whatever was about to happen, so he spurred his animal forward.

"Come on, boys!" cried Slim to his comrades. "We can't let those youngsters tackle this game alone - 'specially when if there's one of the rustlers there may be more. *Pronto!*"

He galloped forward, as did the others, along the new trail that Bud had suggested taking. But Dick was in the lead, and, in a few seconds, was out of sight beyond an outcropping ledge of rock, which narrowed the trail at this particular point.

"Watch your step there, boys!" cried Snake, as he saw What was likely to prove a bad turning. "I don't see how Dick got around it as he did, taking it at the gallop," he went on.

And, as it happened, Dick had not exactly made it, for when Bud and Nort reached the dangerous turn, slightly after Dick had disappeared abound it, they saw no sight of their companion.

"Pull up!" cried Bud sharply. "There's something wrong!" Nort was beginning to think so himself, and he hauled his steed back with such good will and energy that the animal was almost on its haunches.

"Where in the world did he go?" cried Bud.

Nort asked the same question, for there lay the narrow trail before them, running along a ledge, with a shelving bank of shale and sand on one side and a towering face of rock on the other.

Snake Purdee raced at such speed around the turn, in spite of his own admonition to the boy ranchers, that the cowboy nearly ran down Bud and Nort.

"Where's Dick?" cried Snake, at once aware that the stout lad was not in sight.

"He's vamoosed - somewhere," said Bud. "Maybe he met-up with that Greaser and -"

At that moment, however, there came a cry, unmistakably of distress, seemingly from some distance ahead and down below the high and narrow trail on which the party had come to a halt.

"There's Dick now!" cried Nort, recognizing his brother's voice.

"Where in the world is he?" asked Bud, looking about.

In answer Snake pointed down the sloping bank of shale and sand, and there, at the bottom, was Dick, half buried in the soft material, and his horse, with twisted saddle, was standing near by, looking rather the worse for wear. And if the countenance of the animal had been visible it would doubtless have shown pained surprise.

"What's' the matter? What you doing down there?" called Nort to his brother, as Dick proceeded to extricate himself from the sand and shale that covered him almost to his neck.

"You don't s'pose I'm down here for fun, do you?" floated up the somewhat sarcastic answer. "I came around that turn too fast and the horse just sat down at the edge and slid here. It's lucky I'm not killed!"

"It sure is!" agreed Slim. "You want to take a strange trail easy, boy. Are you hurt - or your horse?"

Dick was about two hundred feet below them at the foot of the slope. He got up and limped over to his animal.

"Guess he's all right," was the reply.

"How about you?" asked Bud, for Dick had followed the real westerner's habit of looking first to his steed.

"Oh, I'm scratched up a bit, and lame," was the rueful reply, "but I guess nothing is busted unless it's one of my girths."

The others watched him, while he straightened his saddle, which had slipped around under the horse.

Then Dick called up:

"It's all right. I can ride him, I reckon," which he proved by vaulting into the saddle.

"How am I going to get back up there, though?" he asked. "It's as slippery as an iceberg." "You can't get up," Snake called down. "Don't try it. The trail up here goes along the same direction as the one down there. Keep on it until we join you."

Which Dick did, his pony, fortunately, proving to have suffered no injuries in the unexpected slide down the hill. And thus, by a narrow margin, was an accident diverted. For had the slope down which Dick plunged, because of taking the turn too suddenly, been of rock, both he and the horse might have been badly hurt, if not killed.

"Keep a lookout for that Greaser," called Dick up to his chums above him.

"I don't believe you saw any," retorted Slim. "There aren't any signs of him here."

Nor were there, though the cowboys made careful scrutiny. And afterward Dick admitted that he might have mistaken the fluttering of a bush for the hat of someone he thought a member of Del Pinzo's gang. In a short time the upper path merged into the trail below, and Dick rejoined his friends, exhibiting some scratches sustained in his perilous slide.

Together the posse rode on, making a trail back to the main defile, and out of the one down which the Greaser and his gang had turned, where they had been

Willard F. Baker

discovered by Dick. And then Bud's prediction came true. The sun, which never shone directly into the main canyon for any great length of time, began to set, bringing gloom into the defile long before it would make its appearance on the level country up above.

Seeing the gathering darkness, Slim advised calling a halt, and this was done several miles beyond the place where the last trace of the stolen cattle had been observed.

"Shall we camp here!" asked Bud, deferring to the foreman, as was natural under the circumstances.

"We've got grass and water," Slim remarked, indicating a spring toward which, even then, some of the horses were hastening. "Water for the ponies and us, grass for the animals, and there ought to be some grub left."

"There is," said Snake Purdee, who had assumed, or been given (it did not much matter which) the office of commissary. "We brought along plenty."

"And we may need it before we reach the end of the trail," remarked Bud. "I don't believe it's going to be easy to find where those cattle disappeared to."

"There's only two ways, or at th' most three, in which they could be kept away from us," said Slim, as he slid from his saddle.

"What are they?" asked Dick, who, like his brother, was always eager to learn from a true son of the West, such as was the foreman of Diamond X.

"Well," Slim resumed, "they've either been driven down some side passage, or gorge, such like as we found Del Pinzo in, or they were back-tracked to th' open an' driven off there th' same night they was run off."

"That might be," admitted Bud. "I didn't think of a back track."

"Well, I did," Slim said, "but the signs of it was so faint I passed it up."

A back trail, I might explain, is where an animal, or several of them, or even a human, for that matter, turns and retraces the way first traveled. A fox, fleeing before the hounds, will often do this, and as the scent does not indicate the direction in which Reynard is running, the dogs are often deceived.

But in the case of the fox the imprints of the animal's paws are so light that perhaps only with a microscope could it be told when he had "back-tracked." Except, of course, in some place where soft mud might retain the impression of both trails.

In the case of a large body of cattle, also, though the scent would not be relied upon, it would be difficult for the casual, or, in some cases, even the trained observer, to say where the herd had been turned and driven back over the same course originally taken.

Thus pursuers would be baffled. And when to this is added the fact that the floor of the gorge was of rock, in the main, which did not take, or retain, any impressions, the puzzle was all the more difficult to solve.

"Well, we'll see what happens in the morning," observed Bud, as preparations for the camp went on.

The usual watches were set that night, two of the posse being constantly on guard. It was rather nervous work for the boy ranchers, especially Nort and Dick, as they started at every chance sound which seemed to echo so loudly in the darkness. And once Dick, who was taking the tour of duty with Yellin' Kid, suddenly fired at an object he saw moving.

It was only a luckless coyote, as was evidenced by the howl of pain that followed the report of Dick's gun, and then the night was made hideous and sleepless, for the time, by the chorus of weird howls from the other slinking beasts who were hanging about, hoping for something to eat.

However, it was nearly morning when Dick did his shooting, and a little later they all turned out for an early breakfast, the odor of the coffee and sizzling bacon producing an aroma finer than that of the most costly French perfume.

"And now for the day's work!" exclaimed Bud, when they were once more ready to set off on the trail.

"And may we find something!" was the fervent petition of Dick.

Off they started, refreshed by the night's halt and eager for what lay before them.

I shall not weary you by a recital of all the minor incidents of the day, how they found many false trails and leads, several of which at first seemed promising, but all of which led to nothing.

It was Bud who made the real discovery which, eventually, led to the solving of the mystery. Bud had alighted from his pony, when the halt was made for the noonday lunch, and was climbing up the side of the rocky hill which extended for miles and formed one wall of the gorge.

"Looking for gold?" asked Dick, as he saw his cousin pick up and examine several rocks.

"Sure!" was the laughing answer. "Might find the bones of another Triceratops, too!"

Bud reached forward to pick up something else, and a rock slipped from beneath his foot. He had been resting heavily on it, and the sudden lurch threw him backward. To save himself he clutched at the nearest object, which happened to be a bush growing in the side of the hill. For a moment it seemed that this would save the lad from at least sliding down the declivity, but the bush was not deeply rooted and, in another moment pulled out in the ranch boy's hands. He flung up his arms, and almost toppled over backward, but managed to throw himself forward, and then he slid down several feet.

"Hurt!" called up Dick, ready to hasten to his cousin's aid.

"No, but my shoes are full of gravel. Next time I come up a place like this I -"

Bud suddenly ceased speaking, and began to scramble up the side of the shale-covered hill almost as fast as he had slid down. Then, as he reached the place whence the bush had pulled out he seemed to be looking into some crevice or opening.

A moment later he turned, looked down on the party gathered in the defile below him, and shouted:

"I've found 'em! I've found 'em! Here they are, in one of the queerest places you can imagine! Come up here and look!"

CHAPTER XXIII

THE FIGHT

Scrambling up the side of the gorge, slipping and sliding back, almost like the frog in the well, Dick, Nort and the cowboys reached Bud's side. He maintained his footing only by constantly working his way upward, for the shale, at this point, was almost like fine sand, and kept slipping down, taking the boy rancher with it. But there were bushes growing here and there, and by holding to these, taking care not to pull them out by the roots, Bud managed to stay about where he had been when he made the amazing discovery.

For it was an amazing discovery, as all the others admitted when they reached his side, and looked through the fissure which had been disclosed when Bud pulled out the big bush by which he tried to save himself a fall.

"What is it?' cried Nort.

"And where are they?" demanded Dick.

"It's our cattle! They're inside there - a place like a football stadium only there aren't any seats," explained Bud, breathlessly. By this time he was surrounded by

Willard F. Baker

the others, all maintaining a precarious foothold in the shifting shale. And what they saw caused them all to join with Bud in wondering amazement.

For there, in what was a great natural bowl of the earth, with partly sloping green sides, and with a floor covered by grass, with a pool of sparkling water in the centre, were the missing cattle! The whole of the big herd that had been driven away from Happy Valley was there, it seemed. There they were, in that vast, natural amphitheatre with food and water at hand, and, apparently, as content as when they grazed on the range of the boy ranchers.

"By all the rattlers that ever rattled!" cried Snake. "We sure have found 'em!"

"And they're all right, too!" added Yellin' Kid, as he gazed through the crack which had been opened when Bud pulled out the bush. For it was only through the crack that they were able to view the steers contentedly feeding and drinking within that vast bowl. That is what it was - bowl much more immense in size than the one where Yale battles with Princeton and Harvard. More immense than the Palmer Stadium at Old Nassau. The walls towered higher, and it was greater in diameter. It was almost a perfect bowl in shape - that is as perfect as so natural a formation could be.

"But how did the cattle ever get in there!" exclaimed Nort.

"And how are we going to get them out?" asked Dick.

For it seemed, at first sight, that there was no entrance or egress. And certainly nothing could get in over the top, or out that way. For though the sides of the great, natural bowl were green up to a certain distance, beyond that, and between the rim and a point half way down, they were almost perpendicular in straightness. And, being of rock, they would, it seemed, afford scarcely a foot or hand-hold for the most expert "human fly."

"There must be a way in," declared Slim.

"And out, too," added Yellin' Kid. "Those rustlers never would have driven th' steers in here unless there was some way of getting 'em out."

"But what is this place, anyhow!" asked Nort. "It looks like the Yale bowl, but it never could have been built by man."

"It wasn't," said Bud. "It's the crater of an extinct volcano. It has been filled up, with land-slides, probably, and the winds and the birds have brought grass seeds here, year after year, until it makes a regular corral for cattle. There's water, too, which isn't surprising. That's what it is, an old volcano crater. I heard there was one around here, but I never had time to look for it."

"Yes, I've heard of it myself," admitted Slim, "but I didn't think it was like this. Let's have another look."

Dick and Nort moved aside to give the foreman a place of advantage, and when he had looked through a spot where the crack was wider he said: "I see where they can get th' cattle out. Here, take a look, Bud," and Slim handed the ranch lad a pair of field glasses that had been brought along in case of emergency. They were of value now.

"Down at th' far end, and a little to the left of centre," Slim directed Bud's gaze. "There's a sort of fence of trees piled up. That's th' entrance all right - or one of 'em."

"You're right!" agreed Bud when he had taken a careful observation. "But is there more than one!"

"Must be," said Slim. "The rustlers never drove th' cattle in away around *there*. They sent 'em in from *this* end. Th' trail ends right here, an' it's here where th' rustlers drove th' cattle in."

"But where?" asked Bud. "There isn't a sign of an opening!"

"Because they closed it after them," went on the foreman. "I begin to see it now. There must have been a break in the wall of the old crater right about here. They drove th' cattle in an' it was an easy matter t' let some of th' dirt slide down an' fill it up again. Let's take a look with a view t' seein' if I'm right." It is easier to find a clue when you know just what you are looking for. And it did not take long for the experienced eyes of the cow punchers to discover where earth and shale from above had been recently dislodged and allowed to slide down to cover what must have been the same sort of natural opening into the side of the wall as that at the far end, closed by a fence of trees. This was to keep the cattle in without men being needed to ride herd.

"Yes, it does look as if they'd taken 'em in here," said Bud, when it was found that the trail of the steers led to the foot of the crater wall, where all signs stopped. "If we had looked up a little, instead of sticking so close to the ground, we might have seen this clue before."

"All in good time," observed Slim. "The question is, now, how can we get in there?"

"It will be easy enough," suggested Nort. "All you'll have to do will be to enlarge the crack we looked through."

"That's all right for us getting inside that crater," observed Dick, "but what about our horses? They can't scramble up there."

"Then what can we do?" asked Bud. "Ride around to the other entrance?"

"That would take too long," answered the foreman. "I fancy that Del Pinzo and his gang are on their way to this natural corral now, t' drive out th' cattle they stole from us. We've got t' get ahead of 'em!"

"But how?" Bud wanted to know.

"I think we can dig out enough of th' shale an' dirt they slid int' th' opening, so that we can get th' horses through," Slim answered. "We ought t' have shovels, but we can use sticks t' dig with. It will take longer, but it's the best we can do."

Little time was lost in putting this plan into operation. With a hatchet, which formed part of their camp equipment, some strong poles were cut from one of the few trees that grew on the slope of the gorge, and with these digging operations began. It was slow work, but many hands were engaged and soon an opening was made so that entrance could be had to the original crack in the rocky side of the bowl. For it was by this crack that the cattle had been driven in. And the crack had only been partly filled with broken rock and earth to conceal it from view.

"Yes, they did come in this way!" cried Bud as he and the others urged their horses through the opening and into the bowl proper - the crater of the extinct volcano. "Look, plenty of signs!" There was no doubt of it. The rustlers had driven the cattle into the defile, hazed them along until they reached the opening into this great natural hiding place, and then the rest was easy.

The animals had been run into this solitary place, passing through the narrow, fissure-like opening in the rocky wall, a crack similar to, but larger, than the opening through which Bud had made his discovery. Then shale and dirt had been started, in a miniature avalanche, down the side of the slope, effectually hiding the means by which the cattle were secreted away.

"No wonder we thought an airship had been used," commented Dick.

Before them lay the vast crater of the old volcano, inactive for centuries. Nature had covered the hard lava with a layer of soil in which grew rich grass. And nature had further made the place an ideal corral for cattle by supplying a large spring of water. It was a "rustler's paradise," to quote Slim Degnan.

As the boy ranchers rode into the amphitheatre, the cattle at the far end, and in the middle, stopped grazing to look at them.

"We're friends of yours!" called Bud, waving his hat in the joy at finding his lost stock.

"Yes, but here come some fellows who aren't!" shouted Yellin' Kid.

"Where?" asked Bud, quickly.

"There!" Kid pointed to the far end of the crater, if one may use the word "end" in referring to a circular bowl.

The cowboy posse saw, riding at top speed into the great depression, a crowd of men, who, as they came nearer, could be recognized as the Del Pinzo gang. The Greaser leader was not in evidence, however.

"They're after the cattle!" cried Nort.

"Well, they won't get 'em without a fight!" shouted Bud.

He drew his weapon, an example followed by the others, and as the two parties, one representing law and order and the other the wild, reckless element, started toward each other, the fight began.

Willard F. Baker

CHAPTER XXIV

A DESPERATE CHANCE

"Come on, fellows; Come on!" yelled Bud, as he clapped his heels against the sides of his pony and rushed toward the rustlers. "Give 'em all they got coming!"

"We're with you!" cried Nort.

"A fight to the finish!" shouted Dick.

The boy ranchers had their weapons out, as, indeed, had every one of the following cowboys. Nor was Del Pinzo's gang a whit behind in this, though their lawless leader did not seem to be present. The sun gleamed on the flashing ornaments of silver worn by some of the Mexican Greasers as they rode to the fray.

"Don't ride too far, Bud!" called Slim, for the boys were inclined to be reckless.

"We've got to ride 'em down or they'll have all the cattle out of that far opening before we get there!" Bud answered. And, as he replied he fired one shot in the air, over the heads of the enemy. For Bud bore in mind his father's injunction, not to shoot to wound unless it was absolutely necessary. And Bud thought perhaps a strong show of force would awe the rustlers, causing them to retreat.

However, they were in too strong force for this. And as the boy ranchers and their friends rode on into the vast, natural, volcanic bowl, and were able to take note of their foes, they saw that the rustlers outnumbered them two to one.

Bud's shot - the first of the fight - was the signal for general firing, though, as usual in such engagements, the initial fusilade was wild on both sides; mercifully so, it seemed ordered, for no one was hurt by the opening volley.

"There's going to be a hot time!" shouted Yellin' Kid, as he spurred forward. "And I don't see th' skunk that spoiled my hat! Where is he?"

"Del Pinzo would rather his men'd get th' lickin's!" answered Snake. "He's hidin' out, I reckon."

"I'd like to find his hole!" said Yellin' Kid.

The clashing forces were nearer each other now, with the bunch of Happy Valley steers in between, but off to one side. In order that you may better understand what follows, and the positions of the contending parties, I will explain the situation briefly.

The boy ranchers and their friends had ridden in on what I might call the north end of the volcanic crater, in which bowl the rustlers had hidden the cattle. The opening by which the cattle had been placed in the bowl had been closed by a slide of dirt and shale but this had been partly cleared away by our friends so they could ride through the crack.

At what may be termed the south end of the crater was a larger opening, wide enough, in fact, for several horsemen to ride abreast or a large herd of cattle to be driven through. This opening had been roughly fenced off to keep in the cattle. And it was through this opening that the rustlers had ridden, advancing to meet the force of the boy ranchers coming from the north.

The cattle had been feeding in the centre of the bowl, but as the two parties began the fight, the steers drew off to the west. It was evidently the intention of the rustlers to take out the cattle if possible. Whether they could succeed in driving them away in spite of the pursuit of the rightful owners, or whether they hoped to hide them in some other secret place did not develop.

At any rate, here were the two contending parties racing toward each other, and firing as they galloped forward. And when they were all out in the open it was evident that the rustlers far outnumbered the boy ranchers and their friends.

One thing, however, was in favor of Bud and the others with him. They had advanced farther into the bowl than had the rustlers, and were past the centre when the actual fray began. Using the illustration of a football game, to which I am tempted because of the location of the fray, I might remark that the ball was now over the centre line and well into the enemy's territory. It was up to Bud and his followers to rush it over for a touchdown.

But the rustlers were not going to give up without a

sharp fight. They had come to take away the cattle, and this they now endeavored to do. Several Greasers separated from the main body and began to circle around with the evident intention of cutting out a bunch of steers, to drive them to the larger opening, where the fence had been torn down.

"We've got to stop that!" shouted Slim. "Here, Snake, you and Kid ride over and see what you can do!"

The two cowboys, shouting at the tops of their voices, wheeled to one side and started toward half a dozen Greasers. The odds were not so great as they seemed, for right and justice were on the side of the cowboys.

Suddenly Dick, who was riding between Bud and Nort, gave a little cry, and his weapon dropped from his right hand, on which a spot of blood appeared.

"Hit?" asked Nort.

"Only a scratch," Dick answered. He halted his pony, snatched his neckerchief off and, with the help of his brother, bound up the wound. It was decidedly more than a scratch, being a deep cut where a glancing bullet had hit, and Dick's hand would be out of commission for some time.

"But I can fire with my left," he added, a feat to which he was equal, "and Star guides by knee pressure." He was riding a pony he had taught to obey directions by means of pressure of the cowboy's knees on either side. And Dick had been practicing left hand shooting for some time. His gun restored to him, he rode on with his brother and cousin.

With sudden yells, accompanied by as sudden a rush, a band of the Greasers now rode straight for Bud, Dick, Nort and some of the Diamond X outfit with our heroes. So fierce was the attack, and in such numbers, that there was nothing for our friends to do but retreat, for the time being at least.

This attack took place in a part of the bowl where there were a large number of immense boulders scattered. Seeing that these formed a natural protection, or breastwork, Bud called to his cousins and the men to get behind the stones.

"Make the horses lie down!" was his advice. "We'll fight Indian fashion!"

And, at this point, at least, this became the style of the battle. The Greasers rode fast, endeavoring to cut off Bud and his party, but the latter reached the haven of rocks first, and with the horses on their sides, positions the steeds were glad enough to assume, doubtless, the advantage was on the side of the boy ranchers.

They were protected by rocks, from behind which they could fire, while the enemy was in the open. But the enemy far outnumbered our friends, and the latter, for the time being, were in the position of persons besieged.

For, no sooner had the Greasers seen what was the object of Bud and his followers, than the lawless ones took such small shelter as they could find, some behind their prostrate horses, and began firing at the boy ranchers' party. And as the renegade Mexicans were, in a number of cases, armed with rifles, the odds against Bud and his chums were increased. True, the Greasers were not good marksmen, but a rifle in the hands of even a poor shooter is often more than a match for a .45 revolver in the hands of an expert.

"Pick 'em off!" cried Bud, as bullets zinged their way in among the rocks behind which he and his friends were hidden. "Pick 'em off, but don't expose yourself!"

This was good advice if it could have been followed, but to fire effectively it was necessary for those of the Diamond X outfit to take aim over, or to one side, of the rocks, and when this was done, some part of the body was exposed. At such times the watching Greasers fired.

It was now an actual state of siege as far as Bud and his immediate companions were concerned, and they were outnumbered. Several of Bud's party, including Nort this time, had been slightly wounded. But, in turn, they had wounded some Greasers, too, one vitally, as was learned later.

Meanwhile, Snake and Kid were having their own troubles with the party of Greasers they had been sent off to intercept and prevent from driving off the cattle. More Mexicans had joined their comrades, and Kid and Snake were obliged to beat a retreat, joining Slim and his forces, who were fighting the main, and larger body of rustlers.

And it was while these two separate fights were going on, and while the Greasers that had forced Kid and Snake to retire were gathering together a bunch of cattle to drive out of the main opening, that Dick, who was readjusting the bandage on his hand, saw something that made his heart sink.

This was a sight of another body of Greasers riding into the bowl from the south end - a body of Mexican horsemen led by Del Pinzo himself.

"I guess it's all up with us now," said Dick to his brother, calling the latter's attention to the reinforcements of the enemy. "That's what that half-breed was hanging back for. He wanted to get us well mixed up, and now he'll drive off the cattle."

"Whew!" whistled Nort. "It does look that way. What we going to do, Dick?"

The two brothers were behind a great boulder, off to one side. Bud and some of the cowboys were replying to a brisk fire on the part of the besieging Greasers.

For a moment, after having tied the bandage on his hand, Dick did not answer. Then, as if an inspiration came to him, he said:

"It's only a chance, Nort, and a desperate chance at that. But maybe we can do it! Did you ever read Kipling's 'Drums of the Fore and Aft'?"

"Sure! But what's that got to do with this?"

"A lot. You and I are going to be the 'Drums' and these are going to play the tune," and he tapped his .45. "Come on," he added, motioning to his brother. "As I said, it's a desperate chance, but it may do the trick!"

CHAPTER XXV

LIEUTENANT WAYNE

Not to mystify you, when there is no need for it, I will say that the scheme Dick had hit upon was simple enough. If you recall Kipling's famous story you know that two drummer boys, of a British regiment in India, when the main body was being defeated by a horde of natives, slipped quietly off to one side, and, by hiding behind rocks, played the fife and beat the drum to such advantage that the heathens thought another regiment was approaching to take them in the rear, while the British force was so heartened by hearing the familiar strains that they rallied, the retreat was stopped and the day won.

Dick and Nort had no fife or drum, and, if they had possessed those instruments, it is doubtful if they could have performed on them with any credit to themselves.

Each of them was slightly wounded, but they possessed their guns and had a plentiful supply of ammunition, and it was Dick's idea to use this. "We'll slide out, crawl along that gully there," and he pointed to Nort the one he meant, "and we'll take 'em on the flank. By keeping behind the rocks, and firing fast, we can make 'em think, maybe, that another force is coming."

"You well said it - *maybe*," murmured Nort. "But at that, the idea isn't so bad. They may hold us here all day, and with Slim and his bunch having their hands full, it looks as if the cattle would be driven off."

For while some of the rustlers were holding Bud and his band in check behind the rocks, and while others were fighting Slim and his cowboys, still others were driving the cattle toward the opening in the old volcano bowl. It was Dick's idea that if by a cross fire on the part of himself and his brother, hidden among the rocks, they could scare away the band besieging Bud and his friends, a diversion might be created which would rout the enemy. At any rate, it was worth trying.

Bud was busy, as Nort and Dick slipped off, tying a bandage on the arm of one of the cowboys who had been shot. And the brothers were glad to try their desperate venture unnoticed, for they did not want to explain. And they did not want to be observed going away, as it looked a little like desertion in the face of the enemy. But, for the time being, there was a lull in the fighting. The Greasers who had been holding Bud's force behind the rocks, had quieted down. The fighting between Slim and his cowboys out in the open, however, was going on fiercely, and several had fallen on both sides.

Once Dick and Nort were down in a gully, off to the right of the rocks behind which the band had taken shelter, the eastern lads were screened from observation, both by their friends and by the Greasers.

"Cut along, North!" advised Dick, and, in spite of their wounds, the boy ranchers ran in crouching positions, their guns in readiness.

It did not take them long to reach a point which they regarded as favorable for the trick they were going to play - for it was nothing more nor less than a trick. If they could succeed, by quick firing, in deceiving the enemy, and causing a retreat, a sudden rush on the part of Bud and his friends might turn the scale.

"All ready?" asked Dick of his brother, as they reached some sheltering rocks on the flank of the party besieging Bud.

"Wait until I lay a lot of cartridges ready on the ground. It will be easier to reload them."

"Good idea. I'll do the same."

It was rather awkward for Dick, with his wounded right hand, to reload his gun, but he could manage after a fashion, though not so well as Nort, whose hurt was in his upper left arm. The lads saw to it that their weapons were ready, with a goodly supply of cartridges in front of them. Nort looked across at Dick, behind the sheltering rock, and at a nod from the latter they both began firing.

The effect on the Greasers, poorly screened as they were, was instantaneous. Several leaped to their feet and turned in surprise toward the sound of firing on their flank. These made good targets, and by firing at them Dick and Nort brought more than one to the ground.

Bud and his companions, hearing the firing in a new direction, where, as yet they did not know they had supporters, were also taken by surprise, but it was of another nature.

"Come on! Rush 'em!" yelled Bud, when he had looked around, and, missing Dick and Nort, guessed what had happened. "We've got 'em in a cross fire now! Rush 'em!"

But the Greasers, disheartened by the firing of Dick and Nort on their flank, did not stop to be rushed. Those who were able leaped up and ran toward their horses, which had strayed off to one side. Bud and his party emerged from behind the rocks, firing as they rushed the enemy.

"This is the stuff, Dick!" shouted Nort, as he reloaded his gun and sent another fusilade of bullets into the ranks of the now retreating Greasers.

"I'm glad it worked!" remarked the proposer of the Kipling scheme. "Now we can go help Slim and his bunch. They're having trouble!"

Indeed the tide of battle did seem to be turning against the foreman and his forces. They were outnumbered, and had lost several cowboys, by wounds if not by death - just which it was impossible to determine then. And, meanwhile, the other Greasers, under the leadership of the wily Del Pinzo, were hazing the cattle toward the main entrance.

"Good work, boys! Great work!" Bud greeted his cousins with as he rode out to meet them, when the besieging Greasers had been routed by the cross fire of the two lads. "How'd you think of it?"

"It was Dick," spoke Nort.

"It was Kipling!" Dick answered.

"Get mounted and join us!" Bud requested. "We've got to help Slim!"

This was evident, as the foreman and his cowboys were now hard pressed. But as Nort and Dick rejoined Bud, having leaped to their saddles they, as well as the others from Diamond X caught sight of something which, for the moment made them sick at heart.

For the sight was that of another body of horsemen riding into the old volcano bowl. On they cantered, the sun glinting on their arms.

"More of Del Pinzo's rustlers!" burst out Bud. "We may as well give up! They're too many for us!"

But he did not pull rein, intending it seemed, to fight it out to the bitter end. A cry from Dick was the cause of wonderment. He pointed to the new body of advancing horsemen.

"Look! Look!" Dick shouted. "Those aren't Greasers! They aren't rustlers or Del Pinzo's gang! They're United States troopers! By all the jack rabbits that ever jumped we've got the rustlers now! The United States cavalry is on the job!"

And a moment later, as the notes of a bugle gave a musical order, causing the advancing troop to deploy to right and left, it was evident that the tide of battle had turned in favor of the boy ranchers and their friends.

For the newcomers were, in reality, a troop of United States regulars, and with a dash and vim, exceeded nowhere in the world, and among no other fighters,

Willard F. Baker

this band of grim-faced men entered into action. Carbines were unslung and their short and ugly bark was added to the din.

"Come on, fellows!"

"Now we've got 'em!"

"Over the line!"

"Touchdown!"

These were only a few of the excited shouts of the boy ranchers themselves, while the cowboys of Diamond X riding into the fray with new hearts, sent up their shrill, yipping yells. It was all over then but the shouting, so to speak. The Greasers were fairly trapped - Del Pinzo and all his gang. In vain they attempted to ride around and escape by the main entrance. But the troopers had stationed a guard there, and the bowl was "bottled up." One or two Greasers, sneaking around to the north, did manage to escape through the crack by which Bud and his friends had entered, though the main body was captured and the cattle saved.

"Whew, but that was hot work!" commented Bud, toward sundown, when the rustlers had been caught, disarmed and corraled under guard.

"You told the truth for once," remarked Dick, whose wound had been rebandaged by the surgeon accompanying the troopers.

"And I guess this is the end of Del Pinzo," remarked Nort, for the outlaw Greaser half-breed had been caught red-handed, so to speak.

"I hope so," mused Bud. "But we paid a price for it."

"And so did they," observed Slim. "We accounted for quite a few, but I'm sorry for our boys." Several of the Diamond X outfit had been grievously wounded, and one was killed outright. But the casualties on the side of the enemy were greater.

The fight was over. The cattle of the boy ranchers were saved, and the rustlers captured. Tired horses were staked out near grass and water, and while the cavalry established their camp, Bud and his friends began to wonder how it was the troopers had arrived in the nick of time.

"Well, it was more by chance than anything else," said Captain Parker, who was in command. "We'd been on the trail of these outlaws for some time, and finally we saw a chance to corner them. It was due to the work of Lieutenant Wayne that we were able so to effectually bag them here, though. He has been on scout duty in this section for some time, endeavoring to get information so that we might round up this gang."

"Lieutenant Wayne," repeated Bud, wonderingly.

"Yes, here he comes now. He says he knows you boys."

"Knows us!" murmured Dick, as a trooper approached, saluting his superior and smiling at the boy ranchers. "Yes, don't you know me?" asked Lieutenant Wayne, holding out his hand to Bud. "Perhaps if I had on my glasses, you would be better able to -"

"Four Eyes!" burst out Nort. "At least - I beg your

pardon - Henry - er - Mr. Mellon - Lieutenant Wayne!" he stammered.

"Yes, Four Eyes!" was the laughing answer of the trooper. "Those glasses were only fakes! I wore them as a sort of disguise, and very effectual they were, it seems."

"Four Eyes!" gasped Bud. "And were you in the United States cavalry all the while?"

"Yes, on scout, or detached duty," was the answer. "The government has had many complaints of this band of Del Pinzo's rustlers, and we were detailed to put them out of business. I was assigned to go on duty as a cowboy, which wasn't so hard, as I had been one nearly all my life before joining the army. I worked on several ranches, picking up bits of information here and there, and I completed all I needed to get in Happy Valley," he added.

"And we never tumbled!" remarked Dick.

"Glad you didn't!" laughed Lieutenant Wayne, to give him his proper title. "I thought you were suspicious of me, more than once, though," he said.

"We were, after you built that signal lantern on the watch tower - you did do that, didn't you?" asked Bud.

"Yes, but only as a decoy for the rustlers. I managed to overhear some of their plans, and part of their scheme called for a light on the tower when the time was ripe for a raid on your cattle, boys. So I flashed the signal myself, and, indirectly, it led to this capture today. For I joined my troop right after that, and we have been rounding the rascals up ever since.

"We knew they had made a big raid at your place, but we didn't know where they had hidden the cattle until I happened to think of this old crater, which I discovered one day when I was working for you, Bud. So we made our way here and - well, this is the end, I believe," he added, as he looked over at the bunch of miserable prisoners.

"I hope it's the end," said Bud. "We want to get back to business. And I'm sorry we suspected you, Lieutenant."

"Oh, that's all right. In fact, I'm glad you did. It shows I lived up to the character I was supposed to represent."

There is little more to tell. That night, around the campfire many things, hitherto a mystery, were explained. The stethoscope the boys found was the property of Lieutenant Wayne. He had dropped it when paying a secret visit to Happy Valley. He had intended to pose as a doctor to deceive the rustlers, but, on losing the stethoscope he gave up that plan. It is needless to say that he had nothing to do with the robbery at Diamond X, the real thieves never being discovered. Lieutenant Wayne apologized for cutting his way from Bud's tent the night he disappeared after the signal from the tower. This was the only way he could disappear and accomplish his plans, he said. And it was he who had fired and broken the bottle, and had also fired mysterious signal shots, in order to play up to his character of being in with the rustlers.

"Though the bottle-breaking was only a joke I indulged in," he admitted, "I'm sorry it worried you so."

Willard F. Baker

The soldier, of course, had nothing to do with the prairie fire, and who set it, if it was set, was not discovered. Lieutenant Wayne finally recovered his black horse Cinder, the animal having made its way back to Curly Q ranch, where the officer once posed as a cowboy.

The cattle first stolen by the rustlers were not recovered, but it was found that when they seemed they had been spirited off in an airship they had been merely back-tracked and hidden until an opportune time to dispose of them. Del Pinzo's gang was in hiding, waiting for a chance to drive off the main body of steers, when they were surprised by our heroes. Whether Hank Fisher was in with the rustlers was not decided, though suspicions pointed toward him. The outlaws were sentenced to long terms after being captured by the troopers, and their secret meeting place, having been discovered, was destroyed.

After these explanations had been made, it was decided not to try to drive the cattle out of the crater until the next day.

The night passed without incident, though none of the boy ranchers turned in early. They were too excited, and they wanted to talk over what had happened.

The existence of the old crater was not generally known, but Del Pinzo and his rustlers appeared to have the secret of it. They had driven off Bud's cattle, put them into the natural corral and then filled in, with dirt, the only entrance visible from the defile trail leading from Happy Valley. They intended to use the larger opening out of the bowl, to the south, to get the cattle away. But their plans were frustrated.

The next day the troopers drove off before them the discomfitted Del Pinzo and his disheartened followers, Yellin' Kid taking the Mexican's elaborate hat to replace the cowboy's with the bullet holes. Lieutenant Wayne said farewell to the boy ranchers, promising to come and see them again, in his real character.

The wounded were transported as tenderly as possible out of the main egress from the bowl, it being impractical to use the other. And it was from this larger entrance, after the fence had been torn away, that the cattle were driven, by a long winding trail amid the mountains back to Happy Valley. Only a few were lost by the raid, which was the largest ever perpetrated by the rustlers in that part of the country.

"But I guess, now that the troopers have Del Pinzo, and not the local authorities with their flimsy town jails, that this Greaser won't be foot-loose for some time," observed Bud, when, once more, the boy ranchers were back in camp.

"I don't want to hear his name again," murmured Dick, nursing his wounded hand.

"And to think that Four Eyes was working in our interests when we thought him a spy! That was pretty good!" laughed Nort.

"Yes, it all worked out pretty well," spoke Bud. "And do you know what I'd like to do? I'd like Dad to buy that old volcano crater for us. It would be a peach of a place where we could winter a herd of cattle, and have 'em fat for spring selling. I'm going to speak to him about it," he concluded.

Willard F. Baker

"Well, you can speak right now, for here he comes, and your mother and sister, too," added Dick, as Mr. Merkel's auto chugged down the trail from Diamond X.

"Well, boys, I hear you beat Del Pinzo at his own game!" greeted the rancher, while Nell expressed her sorrow at Dick's wound, to the somewhat jealous regard of Nort, whose hurt was more slight.

"Yes, he's where he won't blur any more brands right away," Bud answered. "But it looked like touch and go for a while. The troopers came just in time!"

"Well, you fellows seem to know how to take care of yourselves and the cattle," observed Bud's father. "Guess I'll turn one of my main ranches over to you. What say?"

But the boys did not answer. They were busy eating slices of a large chocolate cake that Nell had brought over. This is reason enough, isn't it? However, the adventures of our heroes did not end with the capture of the rustlers. And those of you who wish to follow them further may do so in the next volume of this series which will be entitled: "The Boy Ranchers Among the Indians; or Trailing the Yaquis." In that volume we shall meet many of our old friends again, and, should Bud permit it, I may tell you about Zip Foster. But with the capture of Del Pinzo, and his rustlers, this book is finished.